SURVIVING
Brooklyn

BOOK ONE OF THE BROOKLYN SERIES

ELIZABETH YORK

Surviving Brooklyn
Copyright @ 2015 by Elizabeth York

First Print May 2015

Editing by L. Hampton at Editing For You

Rosa Sophia

Steve Czach

Formatting: T.E. Black Designs;
www.authorteblack.com

ISBN: 978-0-692-42042-3

Dedication

I dedicate my first novel, *Surviving Brooklyn*, to my husband: without you, this book would not be possible.

To my children: Thank you for being patient and allowing me to finish this book.

To my friends, family, and fans who believed in me and gave me unconditional support.

To the ministers wife who said girls like me would amount to nothing except to be teenage mothers... Look at me now!

Dedications continued...

Dear Daddy,

You have been gone five years now. I love you and miss you every day. I started this book hoping to make you proud by doing something I love.

I finished it today, Daddy. I hope you are happy. I would do anything to hear you say the words, "I'm proud of you," but in the absence of your voice I continue trying to make you proud.

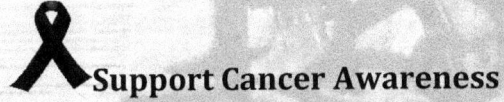 **Support Cancer Awareness**

CHAPTER
One

I STOOD IN THE ENTRYWAY and looked around at the mountains of boxes I still had to unpack. They were stacked three high and lined the cream colored walls in the modest open floor plan. The apartment had everything I was looking for, and the light colored walls contrasting with the darkened hardwood floors made it warm and inviting.

I glanced over and took in my navy blue sectional that was accented with white end tables. It was taunting me with my overwhelming need to relax. I walked over and rubbed my toes on the new gray silk rug that brought the room together. This place was heaven.

The bedroom was large which was perfect since I shoved a majority of my boxes in there. I was able to put my bed on the eastern wall, while my desk and filing cabinets sat on the west. However, the bathroom in my room was my favorite. The cabinets and counter-tops matched throughout the apartment to include his and hers sinks.

I ran a bubble bath, turned on my iPod to Avenged Sevenfold, and set it into the dock, leaving it on random. I placed vanilla candles around the bathroom and slipped my toes into the warm water, then laid back, holding my head barely above the surface as I tapped my foot along to the music.

It was the weekend, and I was going to enjoy every second until I started my new job as the Assistant District Attorney, which means this would be my last work-free weekend. I wanted to use every spare second doing everything I never got to do working for the heinous law firm I had just left. I needed to make fun plans.

As my fingers pruned, I washed up and drained the now-chilled water and stood up in the tub. I grabbed my white towel off the shower hook and patted myself dry before wrapping a towel around my hair.

I collected my clothing from the cream colored antique dresser with its wide mirror, which was a gift from my absentee father. I tried to keep my distance from him because he had a criminal lifestyle, but it didn't stop me from accepting help every now and then.

I had sold my car and most of the furniture I owned prior to moving; the job came with a pay raise, but that didn't help when it was time to put down a deposit to hold the apartment in Tribeca. It was not the cheapest apartment complex; I could have chosen to live in Jersey, but it was safe and there was a subway close by that was a hop-skip-and-a-jump away from work.

After I dressed in my pink pajama shorts and black tank top, I started unpacking boxes. I began in the living room, but got distracted by the case files I was told to look over. There had been a recent increase in unsolved murders, and the last Assistant District Attorney had fallen victim to the same killer.

I took some time to set up my computer and printer so I could scan the files into my laptop; I worked better when I had all the information in the same place. I scanned the photos and the police reports, then glanced over the CSI findings and the FBI profile. This was going to take more than a weekend to cover.

My phone rang and I dropped the folder, instantly apprehensive. I knew I shouldn't be looking at case files when I was trying to relax. I went to the kitchen and grabbed my phone off the island.

"Hello," I answered, without looking at the caller ID.

"I am calling from outside the house." My best friend, Kate, lowered the pitch of her voice, but I knew it was her. She was trying to be creepy, but I found it funny.

"I am answering from inside the house," I replied, trying to stifle my laughter.

"Drinks?" Kate asked. I had already known this call would come. She and her boyfriend had decided to take a break. Eddie had a choice to make and, when he made it, he chose wrong. Kate's mom had been in the hospital, and instead of staying and being supportive, he went to work and then to the bar with friends.

I was by Kate's side that night, and held her hand as her mother passed away. She didn't cope well with Eddie shooting darts at the bar when she needed him to be there for her. Kate had asked him to move out that night, and has been lonely ever since.

"Pick up some Chinese food and wine, then come over here. We can turn up the radio, eat dinner, drink, and dance in our socks while you help me unpack."

Kate immediately accepted my offer, and we hung up. I laid my phone back on the island and walked over to the television. I grabbed the remote and pushed a box out of the way, then walked over to the couch to sit and watch the news.

I watched long enough to see what the weather would be for my first week at work. People claim it is good luck if it rains on your wedding day. I was hoping the logic applied to new jobs as well.

I grabbed the new trash bags filled with packing paper and took them downstairs to the trash container. When I came back up, I found myself distracted by my dock remote. It was new, and I was always terrible when it came to new technology. It took a moment, but I finally figured it out and turned up the radio.

I sat at my desk to begin looking through the case files I had been given. My boss, D.A. Taylor Cross, had given them to me and told me that I had been hand-picked from someone higher up to take over where the last Assistant District Attorney had left off.

Normally, this kind of case would go to whoever had seniority in the office; but, they said they wanted fresh eyes on the case. Not to mention, the detective who was investigating was Mark Stone.

Mark and I had grown up together. We had been best friends all through high school and college. Then when I went to law school something between us changed. He had taken on a serious relationship with a woman named Mary. At that time, my most serious relationship was with a book called Congressional Law from 1862-1962, and I think we just drifted apart.

"Brooklyn?" I heard a familiar male voice call me from inside the apartment. I walked out of my bedroom to see Mark standing in the living room.

"I was just thinking about you," I stated with a large smile. He stood before me in a button-down white shirt and blue jeans. His sleeves were rolled up to show he had a tattoo on his forearm. His detective badge hung from the black belt that matched his boots.

"Good thoughts?" Mark asked with a teasing tone.

His brown hair was gelled, parted off center and arched on the left side. His cobalt eyes blended perfectly with his lightly tanned skin.

"Only the best thoughts for you." I winked to show my playfulness.

He smiled at me, showing me that he still had the same dimples. They formed a line just outside his lips.

"What are you doing here and how did you get in?" I asked, suddenly suspicious.

"Taylor asked me to bring you the rest of the notes from the case file, and you left the door open. Were you trying to attract criminals to get me to come and visit? You know, there are easier ways to get to me."

I laughed and watched as he set down the case file. His smile faltered when he looked at it. Mark was all work and no play when it came to this case; it was taking its toll on everyone. They had no leads, no evidence, and no clues to go off of. The killer was not making this easy for anyone.

"I didn't tell you I moved." I spoke with a silvery tone.

"I am a detective. You didn't have to," Mark replied with a smirk on his face.

"So, what you're saying is that you're a legal stalker?" I countered as I neared him.

"I am whatever you want me to be when you look at me like that!"

Mark lifted me off the floor in a bear hug. I wrapped my arms around his neck and relished the feel of him. An old familiar song came on my iPod as he set me down. He then twirled me into his arms for a dance.

"Do you remember the first time we danced to this?" Mark asked as we swayed to "The Drifters" singing "Under the Boardwalk".

"I do, we were having oldies night at the school and Kevin had just dumped me. You held me in your arms and danced with me all night. You saved me from myself that night." I placed my head on his chest as his hands swayed my hips to the beat.

"I've missed you, Mark," I murmured against his chest as the song changed and he lifted me to swing me in the air.

This was the childish Mark I remembered. As he swung me around and I laughed out loud, I felt at ease. I had even forgotten Kate was coming until I heard her clear her throat.

"Hey, Kate," I stated as Mark put me back on the ground. I was ready to hit the floor from the dizziness. Thankfully, Mark kept an arm on me. When I looked up at Mark, he merely winked, completely unaffected.

"Hi, Kate." Mark held out his hand to shake hers. He had gone from free-spirited and fun to detective as soon as Kate arrived. She finagled the bags she was carrying and saluted him. I could only laugh at her attempt to be funny.

"Hey, guys. I brought Chinese food and I have three bottles of wine. Who is ready to watch Jack Ryan: Shadow Recruit?" Kate asked, holding up the bags.

"Did you get any General Tso's?" Mark asked as he took the bags from her to carry them into the kitchen.

"I sure did, because I knew you would be here," Kate chuckled.

"Shh, Kate, no one is to know I was here," Mark replied with laughter as she tried to follow his hands while they waved in the air in a hypnotizing motion.

"When will you stop these childish games and make a woman out of me?" Kate asked.

"When you start bringing me Chinese food and my slippers."

"She got the General Tso's because it is my favorite, but I share with hot guys and policemen," I replied, putting an end to the giggles rolling out of Kate. Something told me she had already been tasting the wine.

"What category do you put me in?" Mark asked as he tickled my sides.

Feeling like I had something to prove, I pushed Mark across the kitchen with my finger and when he bumped up against the fridge I placed my body right next to him. I hovered my lips as close as I could get to his. Then I slid down him until my mouth came face to face with his zipper and I looked up, licking my lips. I then placed a kiss over his zipper and pressed my body to him as I rose back up. I smiled seductively as I sucked my finger into my mouth.

"When my body against yours starts affecting you, then I will add you to the hot guy column. Until then, you get to stay off that list," I murmured with a smile. Kate was snorting in her drunken laughter behind me.

"That was cruel, woman!" Mark stated with a sly grin, as he went back to setting everything out. All of a sudden, Kate pushed him back against the refrigerator and held a movie case up to his face.

"What the hell are you doing?"

"You could be Chris Pine's doppelganger." Kate slurred her words, and the verdict was in; she was drunk.

"Did you open the wine in the cab on the way here?" I asked Kate.

A nod of the head was the only response. I took Kate's hand and led her to the couch and started the movie for her, then Mark and I took a moment together in the kitchen.

"You have your hands full here. I am going to go," he said. "If you have any questions about the notes in the file, you can give me a shout." Then he handed me his business card.

"Mark, I have your number," I replied, handing it back to him.

"You never use it." He shoved the card back at me. I could not miss the hurt in his eyes when he said it.

The humor between friends was essentially broken. I hadn't called him for anything because he was with Mary. I could not put my finger on it, but I hated her. Maybe it was the way she chewed with her mouth open, or the way she fixed her hair. It really didn't matter because the moment he introduced us, I played the judge and jury and convicted her of being the worst person he could ever be with.

"I'm sorry, Mark. I will call you now that we have this case together."

I wanted to inhale my words back into my mouth the minute I said them. His saddened eyes turned professional, cold, and the anger was clear.

"I need to go." Mark walked to the door and grabbed the knob. I heard a sigh and then he turned back to look at me. "I thought we were friends, and didn't need a case together to call each other."

"We are, and I really have missed you Mark," I stated without using the words I am sorry, but still trying to convey my feelings.

"Well, you know how to find me if you miss me again sometime."

Before I could say another word, he turned his back and left. When I turned back around, Kate was standing by the island.

"What?" I glared at her.

"You got it bad," she said.

"What are you talking about?"

"You want him. You need him. You love him," Kate stated in a sing-song voice.

"We are just friends." I went into the kitchen to clean up. My appetite was gone, along with my happy attitude.

"Yeah, because friends refuse to call each other. You two must be such great friends that you can communicate through telepathy. You both know you haven't come around since he started dicking it to that one chick."

I rolled my eyes and tried to step away, but Kate kept talking. "Look, stick the moral compass in your purse. He wants you. You want him. Now jump on his grill chest and get it out of your system before you explode and start dating a vibrator." Kate finished with a huge smile.

"His grill chest? What does that even mean?"

"You remember my last cookout? Remember that grill I borrowed? The grate was rock hard and made of steel. I imagine his chest would look like that with line after line of rock hard abs. I also think that if I l climbed on top of his chest I would get burned because he is so hot."

Kate tipped the wine bottle up, took a drink and then growled like a tiger at me. She had lost her mind in drunkenness. I shook my head and took the bottle away from her. She pouted and went to the couch to sleep it off, as I headed for my room with the case notes.

Every victim in the file was between twenty-five and thirty. They each had long black hair and blue eyes. They even had the same pale skin and slender body style that I have. I could envision the terror they endured as the photos showed every mark and every bruise; it even showed the blood spatter.

All of the victims were found in different locations, but they were all found the same way. They had their hair styled like 1950s movie stars. Their make-up was flawless, and their naked bodies were covered in thousands of blue forget-me-nots. Their hands were bound by a thick braided rope, holding a single red rose under the forget-me-nots as if they had been laid in a casket.

The killer took his time in torturing and killing them. He used the same precision and diligence in killing them as well as how they appeared after death. Every stab wound was done with surgical precision to inflict the most pain without causing death, then it was stitched back up before he took their lives.

I laid on my bed with the laptop showing me everything in a slide show. It was like a nightmare I couldn't wake up from. They all looked like me. Single, young, white females with similar characteristics.

Did they choose me because I shared an uncanny resemblance to the victims? I shook the thought from my mind; there was just no way they would have chosen to use someone like me as bait, right? I pulled back my navy comforter and sheet to climb inside. I pulled it back over me, and continued going over the case notes that Mark had brought.

CHAPTER
Two

DREAMING

C LICK CLACK—*THE SOUND OF heels echoing down the hallway. The white marble floors gave contrast to the beige walls. There were mahogany doors about every fifteen feet on both sides of the darkened hallway. Everything matched from one side to the other.*

Click clack, click clack—the sound was growing faster and the doors seem to fly by in the never ending hallway. I ran, looking for a red door. I did not know why it was a red door I needed as I glanced at all the mahogany ones.

Out of breath, growing tired very quickly, I kept running. Feeling as though someone was behind me. The anxiety rose up in my stomach as I ran until exhaustion swept in. Passing door after door, I kept going. Down the hallway, a new sound emerged.

Click clack, click clack—someone else was running.

I didn't stop to examine where the noise was coming from. As the footsteps sped up, I glanced over my shoulder. With nothing in sight, I turned back to scan the hallway. Gasping breaths came as I was growing exhausted. Just when I thought I couldn't run any farther, I saw the red door at the end of the hallway. I ran as fast as I could to reach it; it was no more than fifteen feet away. The sounds of the other person were growing louder, and faster. As I reached for the red door, an arm swung around my waist and pulled me from it. A second arm came around and opened one of the mahogany doors to the side and flung me inside.

Landing on my butt and sliding across the floor, I heard the door slam. Immediately, I turned my head, ignoring the pain to my hip.

"Hello," I called out. Fear paralyzed me to the floor when no one answered. A rush of cold air flew by me, forcing me to turn my face away from the cold to see an elevator in the distance. Total darkness surrounded me everywhere except for the light shining over the elevator.

Click clack—the steps were coming again. I couldn't see anyone but the heels running toward me were growing louder. I looked back at the elevator light.

Once inside, the doors closed on the sound of clicking heels moving faster. The elevator started its journey upward. Wood paneling covered the inside with a white floor to contrast and fluorescent lights that flickered off and on. The elevator reminded me of older elevators they used before they got fancy with windows and decorations. I grabbed onto the wood railing; nausea was enveloping me when the elevator starting speeding up, passing two floors each second.

I knelt to the floor in hopes of holding my composure. The swiftness of the elevator had me ready to hurl; every jar and shift was enhanced by the flickering lights. It was as if the elevator lights were flickering to the beat of a song. I closed my eyes and listened to the cranking gears and passing wind as I was escalated up so many floors.

Finally, the elevator came to a stop on the one hundred and eighty-seventh floor. The doors opened and I stood up and stepped out onto a large platform. There were people everywhere. To the left and right of the platform were ropes to keep visitors from falling into the water. Confused by the sight, I wondered who would have a one hundred and eighty-seven story aquarium inside a building. Maybe I was at some Ripley's Believe It or Not museum. Straight ahead, there was a man on a podium, barking orders and calling numbers out as if it were an auction. His demeanor pulled my focus from the water and the people, and my eyes were solely on him.

The man on the podium reminded me of Jeff Goldblum. The black hair and glasses from his days in Jurassic Park fit this man perfectly. The way he talked was deep and authoritative with a rusty tone to his voice. He was barking orders as people were moving to the left and right of the platform in a rush as he called out the numbers. I had an uneasy feeling and turned to get back in the elevator, but the door was locked. I pressed the light, but it wouldn't come on. A silence fell over the room as I tried to pry the doors apart.

The man at the podium parted the people as Moses had parted the Red Sea. This move left me in the middle of everyone, all eyes on me. As I turned to walk toward the man, he began to speak.

"Step forward, take a number. When your number is called, you answer the questions. Get them right, and take the sky lift up eight floors to your new job on the penthouse floor with me. Get one wrong, and you will be dealt with by my favorite pet, Crystal. Get the second wrong, and you will be fed to the sharks. There has never been a third; but, if it happens and you get it wrong, your soul belongs to me!"

I walked up and took a number from the small side table beside the podium and stepped back.

I looked at my number—187. Taking a deep breath, trying to remain calm.

What is it about these numbers? I hated the number eight. It was always bad luck for me. Everything in this place was eights.

"Where do you want to go, Heaven or Hell?" the man asked from his wooden podium. I sucked in a breath at such a question. A question like that was a test.

"Hell," I declared loudly. The man froze, as well as the other people, and stared in my direction. What had I done? They were all watching me.

"We'll come back to you." The man moved right along, asking others different questions.

Coming to a woman with long blonde hair and sharp green eyes, he asked, "Does the world exist outside your own mind?"

The woman seemed worried as she bit the corner of her lip and fidgeted with her clothes. Her jitters captivated how nervous she was as she fiddled with her skirt and lapels.

"Yes," the woman eventually answered.

Everyone gasped in shock. The man waved a finger over at the water on the left-hand side, and the waves started churning. The woman froze.

"Crystal would like to make your acquaintance. Please step to the left of your own accord." The woman didn't move. I was horrified; watching this circus of events as people ran to grab the ropes.

The churning water had a shadow coming up from the bottom. It was one of the largest shadows I had ever seen. As an enormous albino blue whale came to the surface, I nearly fainted. The whale and the blonde locked eyes.

"It seems she doesn't want to meet you, Crystal," the man said to the enormous whale. The blonde began to stutter but didn't make any actual words. "Last chance to go meet Crystal," the man said.

When the blonde didn't move toward the whale, a smile came across the face of the man at the podium. One nod and the whale went down in the water. I thought the chain of events was over, but was proven wrong a moment later. The whale returned to the surface and rose out of the water. A large wave of water knocked the blonde off her feet and slid her toward the right side. She had finally found her voice.

"No! Please, help me!" She screamed. I grabbed onto a wooden post that held the ropes. As the water pushed against my body, I saw there was a family of great white sharks in the water to the right. Where the hell was I?

The blonde was able to grab the rope and hold on as the whale came up out of the water again. The bystanders holding on were groaning with each new wave that hit them. Some even slipped and fell into the water. The oceanic creatures seemed oblivious to anyone except the blonde who was fighting for her life. My desire to help this woman was strong. She screamed as the sharks nipped at her feet.

I pulled myself up off the post and ran to help her. When I got to the woman, everything seemed to pause. The man cleared his throat and all activities ceased. I held her so she was able to get her footing and climb out. Everyone waited to see what would happen.

"Number one eighty-seven, step forward," the man called out.

"No," I replied, my hands on my hips. As an additional act of defiance, I gave him the finger.

"You will stop and obey me." The man bellowed with anger laced in his words.

"Make me," I replied with determination. The blonde waved me off when I turned back to her.

"Let me help you," I whispered to her.

Instead, she looked to the man at the podium and then back at me. The life left her eyes with one glance at him.

"Save me. Only you can save me now," the blonde said in a monotone whisper. Then she threw herself backward into the water.

I quickly turned my head away from the massacre. The water turned red, hiding the way the sharks tore her body into pieces.

"No," I screamed at the man at the podium. "You don't like the answer, so they become fish food. They get to go in the belly of a whale, next they're torn to shreds by Jaws and his friends in some water tug of war. I will not listen to you. I want to go to Heaven, and this charade stops now!" My words failed me as I came to the front of the podium.

The silence in the room emphasized that they had cleared all the people out. There was only me and him.

"Ahh, number one eighty-seven, you seem to defy me in every way. I have something special planned

for you," the man said. I wasn't about to give up.

"Give those people back their lives and their souls and you can have mine!" I screamed.

A smile lit up his face and with a snap of his fingers, men came and tied me to a cable for the sky lift. Once I was tied, the man nodded at the others, telling them what to do.

"I already own your soul," he said.

The sky lift took me up eight floors by my wrists. I was released and dropped on my butt when I reached a penthouse office. I tried to scream, but my voice had failed me again. The same people I was trying to help were standing before me, dressing me. After they dressed me up like Princess Leia in Star Wars with Jabba the Hut, I was left to wait. Allowing my brain to fill with questions as my stomach churned with nervous anxieties and fear.

The green bra was fastened around my neck and had golden metal embellishments across it. The same metal decorations held up the maroon skirt that was spilt on both sides of my hips. There was a golden bracelet on my arm that looked like a snake. I started to panic when I saw it constricting my arm while moving its head up toward my face.

With a chain around my neck, I tried to think back to how I got here. My fate was now in the hands of the handsome devil, with eyes of coal. He stepped out of the shadows and appeared before me as if he had always been there. He stared at me as though I should be begging for my life. I would never cave.

The man jerked on the chain, drawing me to him. I sucked in a deep breath and gathered every ounce of courage left in my shivering body. I refused to let him see fear.

"Are you ready to join me, one-eight-seven?" He asked with a smirk spreading across his face. "Are you ready to suffer eternity with me?" His snide remarks were turning his face more serious, as if made of stone. When he stopped talking, he armed himself with an emotionless mask that made it impossible for me to follow his thoughts.

He began to change. His eyes turned from black to red, and his skin turned from a pale apricot to a crimson red. I started to see shadows of other people's bodies in his skin, as though he'd consumed them whole and they were showing through, growing larger and larger. Every face I saw was someone I had once known. To add to my horror, I knew they were dead. Those faces were trailing one by one up his body. He was growing bigger, his skin darkening as if he was made of nothing but the blood of others. He grew larger until I was eye level with his thighs.

Once he was full grown, he wasn't a man anymore. He had a dragon face with a long red tail that had a spade shape on the end. He used it to slice my leg open. He watched while I cried from the pain. He watched while I bled on the floor. The same curl of a smile crept across his face. The faces that lined his scaly body seemed to scream out for help. When my attention got caught on one of the faces, he jerked the chain in an upward motion, bringing me face to face with him.

"Do you like dragons?" he asked.

Oh God, I am going to die. I was fighting for my life, struggling for air. I kicked and screamed. I would do anything for him to either end it or let me go. I fought with everything I had in me to realize that, even though the collar clung to my throat and held me up, I was not choking. Fear ravaged my brain as I thought I might already be dead and this was me facing the devil himself. Closing my eyes, I said a silent hopeful prayer.

"You are so yummy," the demon said.

I tried to scream, but his tongue came out and pierced my lips, sliding down my throat, stopping all sounds.

This must be the final touch of my death, I thought. Except he took his tongue out and pulled my body inside out from my neck down. Staring down in shock, I could see my bones on the outside of my body. I watched as he slowly devoured each piece. I couldn't look away as he ended my life bite by bite.

A flicker of light caught my eye. It was my heart beating behind my ribs. My soul lives in my heart. It makes me who I am. If he eats my heart, it will be the end of everything I am. I will be forgotten, a name on a tombstone no one visits. The regrets that plagued me were enough to give me a slight reprieve from what was happening in front of me.

With a man's chuckle coming from the monster's lips, he went for my heart. The pain was excruciating. How I was still breathing was beyond me. Agony and fire had set in. No time to wonder again about how I was alive. No time to think of regrets. There was no relief in sight when he came for me again. This couldn't be the devil because even he would have felt empathy for what I was enduring.

My heart lit up inside his mouth as I watched him chew. Swallowing hard, he jerked me toward him with the chain still in the air. This time he was taking his time moving toward my face. The memories that flashed before me were of my childhood and made me want to weep. He was going to eat all of me until there was nothing left. Would I live in agony inside him forever, or would I die?

Life was full of choices and roads in which to wander aimlessly down. None had shown me this. It wasn't hidden in a valley or at the peak of a mountain. Nothing could have prepared me for the intense agony I felt. Nothing could have prevented me from trying to help the blonde who threw herself to the sharks rather than be eaten by the giant flesh-eating dragon that held me up by a chain.

The agony and pain had no description as no words could describe how awful it felt. The pits of hell would have sympathized with me. I knew how every victim must have felt before he killed them and ended their pain.

The dragon chuckled and asked if I had made my peace with what was happening. I couldn't even respond between the pain from my nonexistent body and the strain from the collar I wore. There were no words or sounds. The dragon threw his head back with a whole-hearted laugh.

"I guess this means I win. This means you won't ever stop me." He growled.

He moved forward so slowly, with lips curling upward to show teeth covered in blood. His mouth looked like the inside of a crocodile's mouth. Tired of the game, he moved in such a fast motion all I could do was try to scream as he bit down on my face.

CHAPTER
Three

"Ahh!" I screamed, fighting my blanket. I was stuck beneath the blanket. My laptop cord had me pinned down. The room was dark and the only light was shining from my laptop as it returned from its sleep mode. I finally got loose and fell to the floor. I rubbed my hands up and down my body for peace of mind that I was still there.

I looked toward the light and saw the gruesome crime scene photos. I had only been on the case for a few days, and it had already gotten under my skin. Could it be because they all looked like me?

"Brooklyn?" Kate flipped on my light. She had fallen asleep on the couch and I had woken her with my screams. She ran for me as soon as she saw me, immediately enveloping me in her arms. She gave me a hug that shattered my emotional hold. I cried on her shoulder. I cried for the victims, and for myself. I always wanted to put away bad men. I wanted to make sure they stayed behind bars, but I never imagined it would feel like this.

"I am all right," I muttered through my tears. Kate let me go and pulled back to study my face.

"You want me to sleep in here?" she asked with a softened tone.

I nodded my head and put all the case material and my laptop on my desk. I took a shower and scrubbed the dream off me. When I returned, Kate was still awake. She had turned out the light, but had brought in my little desk lamps and they were turned on in the four corners of my room. It gave me enough light not to run into any boxes, but was soft enough I would fall right to sleep.

I climbed in the bed, thankful my best friend was there, and fell fast asleep.

THE REST OF THE WEEKEND passed by in a blur of unpacking, drinking, and dancing in our socks. Kate had given up her weekend, except to get clothes out of her apartment to stay with me. I didn't have a repeat nightmare, but I also did not pull out the case file before bed again.

By Sunday night, I felt like I wanted to see my dad, hadn't spoken to him much since he got out of prison. He lived his life as a criminal and I was going to spend mine putting people like him in prison. I wanted to tell him a victim's side of the story. I wanted him to have empathy for those he had harmed. I picked up my phone and called him.

"Lyubov Moya, how are you?"

"I am fine, Nikolas, how are you?" I replied.

"When are you going to start calling me *Dad?*"

"When you start behaving like one." This conversation was off to a rocky start. He would likely hang up on me, so it would be best to say something in person.

"I start my new job tomorrow."

"That is great. Did you get a new law firm?" Nikolas asked, as if he had forgotten where I took the job.

"I took the job with the District Attorney's office. They already have me on the Cut-Me-Not case."

"The one on the news?" my dad asked. His tone was a little off-putting. It almost sounded like he was concerned.

"Yes, that one. I will get to try the case if we ever catch him." I took a breath, and was cautious not to say anything more than what he would learn by watching television. Not only did I worry about confidentiality with my job, but my dad was a convict.

The FBI took pride in the fact they had rid New York City of the mafia. Little did they know, the mafia still resided. They were all employed by my father and his army of idiots.

"Brooklyn, I want you to be very careful with that. Didn't he just kill the last Assistant District Attorney?" my dad asked with concern.

"Yes, I took her spot. Nikolas, I know you have to be worried because you are my sperm donor, but honestly I will be fine. I am working with Mark on it, and he won't let anything happen to me."

Kate took the opportunity to wave at me and let me know she was dressed and ready to go to dinner. I held up one finger to finish my call with my dad.

My dad didn't believe me when I said I would be fine. I got the same speech he gave to his thugs about watching their backs. He worked in a world of criminals, so maybe I should listen, but then again the press release had not even gone out yet. No one knew I had taken over, and I had no threats against me. Being a virgin to this side of the system meant I had no enemies yet. I was sure I would be fine.

I enjoyed the groans my dad conveyed when I asked him to pick me up for lunch from the same office that put him behind bars for most of my childhood. He would just have to deal with the fact that his criminal genes did not leak into me.

I hung up with him and threw on a red rockabilly dress with a black chest-belt and black pumps. I let my black hair flow and applied my make-up. The red dress made my skin look lighter, but it also made my blue eyes pop with color. This was my last night before work began, and I wanted to look my best.

One last glance in the mirror and I turned to leave with Kate. Tonight was going to be fun.

A FEW HOURS HAD PASSED and dinner at Pure Wine & Food had been great. I loved the environment, and Kate loved their vegetarian cuisines. We were walking out to leave when I turned and ran into a hard male chest. It had to be the wine that left me stuttering my apologies as I bent down to pick up my purse. I suddenly felt hot as I brushed against the man handing me my jacket that had also fallen to the ground. I didn't even make eye contact until I had straightened.

"You all right?" Mark asked.

"Yeah, I am good," I stuttered. "What are you doing here?"

"Your dad called me," Mark answered as if it was no big deal.

"Since when do you consort with the enemy?" I asked, letting my distaste for my father shine through.

"When we have a common goal." Mark responded with a smile that lit up his face. My annoyance that my dad had called him was making him laugh, and that irritated me even more.

"What exactly is your common goal?" I placed my left hand on my hip and prodded his hardened chest with my right.

"You," Mark stated nonchalantly. He took my hand in his to keep me from poking him again. Retaining my annoyance was hard around Mark. He made me feel as though I could take on the world with him by my side, and everything would be all right. He made me think I was some kind of an enigma.

"Me?" I asked.

"You." Mark brushed my hair back behind my ear when the wind blew it across my face.

"What about me?" I asked, warmth in my voice. Mark was just that type of person; he could piss me off while making me want to coddle him. It was made worse by his dimples. I was infatuated with his dimples. They added to his character and made him look handsome and mature but with a slight amount of childishness that made him irresistible.

"Invite me home with you," Mark whispered as Kate came upon us.

"Hey, Mark," Kate said, looking down at Mark's hand that was still covering mine. She glanced back up at me and winked. Then her lips moved silently to the sing-song phrase she had said days earlier. Lucky for me, Mark's gaze had not left me, and I was saved from the humiliation of trying to explain what Kate was saying.

"Hi Kate, how are you?" Mark asked without looking in her direction. He was staring into my eyes as if he was waiting to see if I would acknowledge his request from a moment ago.

"I'm great! I am just drunk enough that I am heading to Eddie's." Kate mentioned Eddie candidly, as if he wasn't the soon to be ex-boyfriend.

"Are you serious?" I asked, wondering what was going through her head.

"Yes, I know we have no future together, but that doesn't mean we can't use each other for sex until we are ready to move on."

I closed my eyes so she would not see me roll them with her comment. I wasn't going to talk her out of it. Maybe she needed this to see that he wouldn't change.

"Text me when you get there," I said softly. "Mark, would you come home with me and go over the notes?" I asked, because I had not forgotten what he wanted.

Kate waved goodbye to me, and Mark took my arm as we walked down the street. I noticed a black town car slowly cruising just behind us. People in New York City did not know what traffic laws were, so it wasn't strange to see that kind of car, but it was odd that it was moving so slowly.

I put it out of my mind as we rounded the corner and Mark lifted his arm to hail a cab.

"Remember the last time we shared a cab? Mark asked with a sly grin.

"I remember. I puked all over your shoes, and your girlfriend got pissed when I climbed in your lap so you could make me feel better," I said with a smile to match his.

"I remember I stayed by your side the entire night. I held your hair while you puked. I rubbed your back with the dry heaves. I even got you 'hair of the dog' the next morning," Mark whispered the memory as if it was something that just happened. Then he lifted my hand to kiss my knuckles as he climbed into a cab.

He didn't say a word the rest of the ride to my apartment. I didn't speak either. It seemed like we had a lot to say, but the scary part was saying it out loud. I would eventually ask why he would come at my father's request, but here and now in the back of the cab I was enjoying the silence as he continued to hold my hand.

When we arrived at my apartment, Mark took the keys from my hand and placed his other hand on the small of my back while the doorman let us in. We rode up the elevator in silence, letting the sonata playing through the speakers control the mood. As we got to my floor, Mark took my hand and led me to my door and unlocked it.

Once inside, Mark locked the door and made his way through what was left of my boxes to put my keys on the island in the kitchen. I took a bottle of tequila out of the freezer. Mark stood with his elbow leaning down on the island, watching as I made margaritas. I knew I had to work tomorrow, but one or two wouldn't hurt.

"Why have you been avoiding me?" Mark asked as I turned off the blender. I couldn't pretend I didn't hear it. I guess honesty is the best policy, but I am a lawyer, so unless directly asked I don't share any extra information. I poured my own drink, and decided I could be my own lawyer.

"I wasn't avoiding you," I stated, pouring Mark a drink.

"Yes, you were, and I am not leaving until I know why." Mark drained his glass in one swallow.

"What did my dad call you for?" I asked, trying to change the subject.

"Quid Pro Quo. You answer my questions and I will answer yours," Mark responded. I was seriously ready to kick my own ass because that was the tactic I used whenever I had information he wanted to know. He had turned the tables, and I would die of embarrassment or shame before the night was over.

"Fine! Name the stakes," I declared. I was never one to back down. I was also trying to figure out how to tell him I hated his girlfriend and wanted to watch her drown in my jealousy.

"Whatever is said here, stays here. I will be completely honest with you if you are honest with me. The last time we discussed your dad, you threw a vase at me. I want it on the record that there will be no throwing of items."

Mark grabbed a beer out of the refrigerator and walked over to the couch. It was my turn. I refilled my glass and brought the pitcher with me, then set the pitcher on the coffee table before plopping down on the other end of the couch. I turned myself sideways to face him. I knew he was in detective mode, so I would have to go the honest route and not the lawyer route.

"Mary," I stated, my lips on my cup. I knew he caught what I said, but he was going to make me repeat it anyway.

"What?" he asked, showing his patience was wearing thin.

"Your girlfriend, Mary." I stared into my cup; the liquid was quickly dissipating.

"Why would you avoid me because of her?" Mark asked, appearing confused. I couldn't blame him, it was a valid question. I hadn't even shared my distaste for her with Kate.

"Just because," I answered as I poured another drink. My belly was warm and my head tingled from the effects of the alcohol, but I wasn't drunk yet.

"Explain it to me," Mark stated in a loud manner. He sounded angry, but he looked intrigued.

"I just don't like being around her when she is with you," I answered quickly, "Why did my dad call you?" I wanted to know before he dug any deeper into my heart.

"He asked me to see if you would be willing to walk away from this case. He thought with our history I would be able to talk you out of it." Mark sat silently as I mulled over what he had just said.

"Next time he calls, you can tell him the victims and I are the same. That if I walk away, there is no guarantee they will ever get justice. As long as I am on this case, I won't stop until those women get the justice they deserve so they can rest in peace."

"Did she threaten you?" Mark asked. "Did she do something to offend you? Did you get into an argument?"

He had switched the topic back to Mary. While I was grateful he was not interrogating me, I would not put it past him to stick me in a dark room with a light in my face and take on his detective attitude.

"No, I just don't like her," I said as I stood and walked over to the television stand. I placed my cup down and put my hands on my hips. Keeping my back to Mark, I drew in a deep breath. I knew he had stood up and was closing the space between us. I could feel he was behind me before he touched me.

Mark placed his hand on my hips and turned me to face him. I kept my head down and stared at his black belt. The silver in the clasp had me mesmerized, and I imagined if I continued to stare he would not pry any further.

"Look at me," Mark whispered, his fingers laced with mine on the backs of my hips. He dropped one of my hands when I didn't look up at him, then placed his index finger under my chin and lifted my face toward him. I knew he wanted answers, and he knew I didn't want to confess.

"It's just me. You can talk to me," Mark whispered as I held back the tears that filled my eyes.

"No, I can't," I murmured as the alcohol seemed to disappear from my body.

"Brooklyn, it's just us here. Just you and I. Obviously you have a strong reason. Your eyes are glistening with tears. You can't hide your feelings from me. You wear them out in the open so everyone can see when you are hurt or scared. Let me fix this for you. Just tell me what has you so upset."

I wrestled with the words inside my head for a few minutes. Mark didn't move. Kate once told me the best way to say something that scared you was to blurt it out. Like ripping off a band-aid, the longer you draw it out, the harder it gets.

I looked into Mark's cobalt eyes, which seemed to have a silver lining. The cliché popped into my head about how everyone should always find the silver lining of the cloud, and I was staring into mine. I was scared we wouldn't be able to work together or that things would become awkward. I worried about ruining the friendship we had built over twenty years.

The last time we were together was just a mere two days ago, and I had managed to offend him without even trying. What would his reaction be now? Would he be offended, appalled, or would he utter the words 'were better off friends?'

"Mark, we have known each other nearly twenty years." I pulled back from him to gain some space. It didn't last because I was now against the television stand with nowhere to go, his hardened body only inches from mine.

"Yes, Brooklyn, we have been friends a long time. That doesn't explain it." Mark pushed my hair off my shoulder.

"I am trying to explain," I replied hastily. "In those twenty years, we have grown to be very good friends. You're my best friend. Mark, I—"

"Brookie, just say it. Tell me what it is that has you so flustered. You used to be able to tell me everything," Mark whispered, giving my hips a little squeeze as he closed the gap between us. His warmth enveloped me, and I stared at the silver lining around his cobalt eyes wishing he would look at me the way I always looked at him.

I swallowed loudly and my heart rate increased as Mark stared into me. I could feel him. I could feel the strength and courage that came from being near him.

I can do this. I just have to open my mouth and let the words flow out.

"Mark, I have strong feelings for you."

I did it, I told him. I wanted to do a cartwheel and give myself a high five. I had always buckled under the pressure unless it was in a courtroom, but here and now I had excelled. It was like I was breathing fresh air for the first time in a long time after the words left my lips. Then I realized the hard part had only just begun, that Mark still had to reply. I held my breath as I watched his brows draw together, and his eyes became focused as the words left his mouth.

"What kind of feelings?"

I couldn't run from his question. He was like gravity holding me in place where I belonged. He was holding me against him and demanding my soul to open up and pour my heart out.

"Mark, I have fallen in love with you," I whispered as his eyes burned into me.

"How long?" Mark replied.

"Since the day we met," I whispered softly.

The silence in my apartment was deafening as I waited for his response. Every second that ticked on the clock seemed like hours, and the minutes felt like years. I took a deep breath and began to shelter my heart when Mark placed his finger under my chin to hold my head up.

"Mark, I don't expect anything from you. I was never even going to tell you. I just—"

He placed his finger over my lips to quiet me. He moved his hand to the side of my cheek, and brushed away the tear that flowed. Slipping his other hand behind my neck, he continued to caress my cheek.

My stomach quivered, and my pulse quickened. My body shivered as he neared me. I truthfully questioned how far this would really go until his lips brushed mine.

His kiss was soft and warm. His tongue brushed against my lips, and I parted for him to gain entry into my mouth. I returned his caresses as his tongue invaded me, and I tasted coffee and whipped cream as I felt his fear, his happiness, and even his need in his kiss. More importantly, I felt his love for me. I threaded my fingers in his silky brown hair.

Mark lifted me and set me on the television stand I had been standing against. My margarita glass toppled and shattered on the floor. I would have cared if I didn't have this man between my legs.

I reached for his belt as his velvet kiss stole my breath once more. Every time I thought he was ending the kiss, he came at me again. I was ready to go much further when the phone rang.

First his phone, and then mine. This was not a good sign. Mark pulled his mouth away, but rested his forehead to mine as we caught our breaths. We let the phones go to voicemail. We would deal with it in a minute.

"You should always tell me everything. Stay here. We will discuss this later." Mark pulled his phone from the clip on his belt.

I watched as he put on his shield. When he was on duty, he was Detective Stone and wore an invisible shield around his heart. When he was off duty, he was fun-loving Mark. I adored both sides of him. It felt weird to even say it in my head. I had denied what I felt for so long that admitting it was like coming up to breathe while swimming in deep water. He hadn't said he loved me. He hadn't really said anything. We would have to make sure our friendship would survive, but it would have to wait as the phones rang again.

Mark stood in my doorway as I looked at my phone. Another victim had been found. It was a nauseating realization, but it was time to go to work because the killer had struck again. As I watched Mark walk out the door, I wondered if I would remain inside or go to the crime scene, and let the world see that I had taken over this case.

Was I ready for this?

CHAPTER
Four

I HAD A CAB DROP me off on the corner of 59th and Park. I was standing across the street in front of one of the entrances to Central Park while I watched the scene unfold.

It was like watching a ballet. Everyone was in their place, doing their job, moving in coordination with the leader. I watched, mesmerized, as an officer in a black jacket took photos of a girl who lay lifeless on the ground. The coroner was standing over her, making notes. Mark looked right through me when he saw me. The area was covered in press and cops. The Plaza was having to reroute guests, as the body was outside their door by the Pulitzer Fountain.

Mark turned his back to me and began shouting orders as I walked closer to the scene. I had never been to a crime scene before, but I had an idea of what transpired. Most of the time, the Assistant District Attorneys didn't go to crime scenes, but this was a different kind of case and they wanted to make sure everything was done to the letter of the law. Once we caught the killer, we were never going to let him walk on a technicality.

I came up on the blue police barriers and flashed my A.D.A. badge to get through. I was thankful I had taken the time to change into a pair of skinny jeans and my white button-down. Adding to my look was a pair of white heels. My appearance was just as it should be, and I was hopeful that tomorrow's headlines would not read *Mafia princess visits crime scene* or something even worse.

"Go home, Brook." Mark glared at me as he spoke softly. I nearly missed how irritated he looked because of the tone of his voice.

"I need to see what I am dealing with." I wasn't talking to him as a friend or someone he cared for. I was speaking to him as a prosecutor.

"Two hours ago, you were drinking margaritas. I cannot have you here inebriated," Mark replied.

"Give me a breathalyzer. If I fail, you can book me with public intoxication. If not, step aside and let me do my job."

I tried looking around Mark, but his football player build made it hard to look past him without being obvious. I held my footing and stared back at him. He was used to being in charge at crime scenes, but here and now it was my job to make sure he did his job correctly.

"Do not leave my side, Brook. You step away from me, and I will drag you home and spank your ass for not listening. Once the scene is cleared, I will escort you home." He took my elbow in his hand, and slowly walked me toward the coroner.

They had taken the time to cover the body since my arrival, but they made no attempt to move her. I watched as the crime scene personnel looked over every inch of the surrounding area.

I later saw two FBI agents in the distance taking pictures with their cell phones from behind the barriers. I recognized them immediately. I tugged on Mark and began to walk toward them. Mark altered his course and came along with me.

"What are you two doing here?" I asked angrily.

They had always snooped around my family. One of these men was maybe five-foot-ten, and appeared to be in his late forties, with gray hair and glasses. His name was Special Agent Donnelley. The other was roughly six feet tall, with gray and white hair. Agent Carter.

"We came to see for ourselves," Carter said. "Eventually, the NYPD will call on us. We are ready when the time comes for the NYPD to admit defeat." He snickered.

"You need to leave," Mark growled. He was so sexy when he was serious. I had to break the thought from my mind and find a way to end this without a testosterone war.

I waved over one of the crime scene officers. The young blond was named Chris. He was new to the force and fresh out of college. He looked up to Mark as if he was some kind of a hero. I knew he would do anything for Mark, and that allowed me to take advantage of the situation.

"Detective Stone needs you to bag and tag those agents' phones. The pictures they took are now evidence until we deem otherwise."

Chris immediately turned to the agents and began explaining the need to take their phones as Mark and I turned away. I winked at both agents. This new job may come in handy with men like them.

Mark led me back to the body. The coroner began speaking in a language I could not understand.

I stopped listening as I stared down and saw the victim's blood pooling outside the plastic sheet. The coroner pulled the plastic back to show me the rose she held, her hands bound by rope. Her hair and make-up perfectly styled to be a 1950s model. She was naked and covered in thousands of blue forget-me-nots. Someone had taken the time to dead-head them and use them as a cover for the body.

I knelt down and stared at the face that matched mine. She had the same blue eyes and black hair. Same skin tone, and even the same tiny butterfly tattoo on her ankle. The coroner ran his hand over the victim to close her eyes as nausea rose up in my stomach. A subtle wind blew and a flicker of silver caught my eye as I looked at the flowers. She wore a necklace. Mark and the coroner saw it the same time I did. The coroner moved the flowers lightly, adding light to the necklace on her chest. It was a silver braided rope in the shape of a noose.

I reached my hand into the top unbuttoned portion of my shirt and pulled out my silver necklace.

Mark and the coroner stared as I held it out. It matched hers exactly. It was like looking in a mirror. She was me.

My necklace had been a graduation present from my sperm donor, Nikolas. It was his way of saying being a lawyer was like hanging yourself. While I did not see the same meaning, I wore it every day anyway. I started walking backward as Mark followed. My thoughts clouded as the nausea overwhelmed me. I found myself turning around to face a large group of paparazzi.

"Have you identified the body? Is it the same Cut-Me-Not killer?"

I could not answer any of their questions. I ran across the street and into the park. I stopped and threw up in the trash can just outside the zoo.

The coroner was behind me.

"You all right, dear?" he asked as my dry heaves kicked in.

"She was me," I blurted out as my heart raced. My palms grew sweaty and my head began to ache. I thought I might throw up again, but the coroner had me sit on the park bench and place my head between my knees.

"I understand what you see, but she is not you. You are still here, and she is not. You both have similar items which means you have similar taste. That is all." He gently rubbed my back.

"What's your name?" I should have known before I arrived, but my curiosity got to me before I could think to ask for names.

"James Garie."

I lifted my head from my knees, and reached up to shake his hand. "I am the new nauseously mortified Assistant District Attorney Brooklyn Montgomery," I said as we shook hands. "It's a pleasure to meet you."

"Well, Ms. Montgomery, how do you feel now?" James asked.

"I think I want to go home." I rose to my feet. "Can you tell Mark I will wait here for him to drive me?"

James nodded, and went to get Mark. He wasn't gone a moment when a man walked up.

"You all right, Miss?" he asked, as I hugged my belly from the nausea. The man had an accent I could not place.

"Just a little nauseous. I will be fine, thank you." I took a second glance at this man, as most people in New York City are not nice enough to stop a stranger on the street and see if they're okay.

He had blond hair and dark green eyes. He was very tall, but it was hard to tell how tall from my position on the bench. He had a crooked nose that looked like it had recently healed from a break. I looked down at his hands; he was cracking his knuckles when I saw a dripping dagger tattooed just below his thumb. His black hoodie was out of season for the weather, and he looked like he had mud all over his jeans.

"Miss, I just want to say even though you are feeling ill, you are the most beautiful woman I have ever seen. Your face is truly one of a kind."

Before the chills of danger shivered down my body, he had already walked away. It wasn't long before I saw Mark coming for me with two extra officers and a worried look on his face. I watched as he scanned the area as if the killer was there somewhere.

"Brook, you all right?" Mark asked, reaching down and lifting me off the bench.

"I'm mortified." I wrapped my arms around him, and buried my face in the crook of his neck.

"I am taking you home," Mark declared, as he carried me out of the park and into the black Escalade the police force had just given him.

He piled me into the passenger seat, and buckled me in. I would have spoken out that I was not an invalid; but the way I felt, I wanted the comfort and warmth of someone taking care of me.

UPON ARRIVING AT MY APARTMENT, I discarded my heels. I unbuttoned my long sleeve white shirt and dropped it, revealing the black tank top beneath. Taking my pants off, I walked into the bedroom in my underwear and tank top. I climbed under my comforter and buried my face in the pillow.

"Brook," Mark called out, but I refused to look up at him. "Come on, Brook."

I felt his weight press onto the bed and took a deep breath. Humiliation had invaded my veins after I got sick outside the crime scene. I glanced up to see a smile on his face. Men wouldn't understand humility if it bit them in the ass.

"Go away, Mark," I murmured with my head on my pillow. Instead, he stretched out on the bed so we were eye to eye with one another. He took my hand in his and uttered the words no woman ever wants to hear in bed.

"Do you need me to get you a barf bag?" His laughter was intoxicating, and soon I was giggling along with him. Until I realized we were both laughing at *me*.

"It's not funny. Someone died," I shouted. Mark's laughter halted and his face fell. I don't even know why I blurted that out.

"Brooklyn, I know someone died. It makes the fifth victim since this began. I was finding humor in your humility, not the situation. I would never under any circumstance find it anything other than horrid when someone has their life brutally ripped away from them."

Mark sat up and seemed to argue with himself for a moment. He stood and left my bedroom. Twice, I have said something to piss him off. Perhaps I needed lessons on how to be a good friend.

I stood and grabbed my gray fleece blanket off my computer chair and wrapped it around me. I looked around, but I didn't see Mark. I would have to find a way to apologize to him later. I went to the front door and locked it. When I turned around, the aroma of coffee hit me. I wandered into the kitchen where I found Mark looking in the bottom cabinets.

"I thought you left," I said as he glanced up at me.

"Do you want me to leave?" Mark countered as he rose, holding a skillet.

"Isn't Mary going to get upset that you're out so late?" I hated bringing her up, but I didn't want to cause trouble for Mark.

"I think her husband might have a problem if I called her and asked." Mark turned his back and put the skillet on the stove.

"Her husband? Wait…*what?*" A blush invaded my cheeks. I must have turned a crimson color because it was at that moment I realized I was nearly naked in front of him.

"Brookie, Mary and I broke up over a year ago. You would have known if you used your phone and called me every once and a while." Mark stated with laughter, as he began cutting cherry tomatoes. "You may want to sit down. You look as red as these tomatoes."

I ran into my room and pulled on a pair of drawstring sweatpants. It was midnight, and I should be in bed getting some sleep for my first day at the office in the morning, but with Mark single and cooking in my kitchen I would rather stay up with him and take a sick day.

I finished dressing and walked back into the kitchen. He was making me homemade pasta primavera. It was a family recipe my mom had taught Mark before she died. It was my feel-good food. Mom made it for me whenever I was feeling down or just needed a boost.

"What's the occasion?" I asked as I came upon Mark, who had made me a cup of coffee. I took a seat on one of the island stools and sipped my coffee.

"We still need to talk about earlier tonight, but it can wait until dinner is ready. I want to know about the crime scene." Mark sighed before continuing. "You know I got sick at the first violent crime scene I ever went to. You never get used to it, but you learn how to adapt and overcome it."

Mark stirred the food as the sauce began to thicken. I felt at home with him here, but discussing the crime scene was not something I ever envisioned or fantasized about.

"All the press will write stories about how the new prosecutor could not handle a crime scene," I said. "They will replace me before I even get a chance to try."

Mark leaned over the counter and brushed his thumb across my cheek. He seemed to empathize with me. Then he leaned down and placed a soft kiss on my lips. With the island between us, it was hard to deepen the kiss and I wanted to. I pushed my coffee cup aside and climbed up on the island.

I crawled on my hands and knees over to Mark. With my lips never leaving his, I twisted my body around to hang my legs off the island with him in between them. I threaded my fingers through his hair and poured my emotions into the kiss.

I could taste the Alfredo sauce on his tongue, giving away his inability to control his taste-testing. He pulled me into his waist as a moan left my lips. All at once, he tugged my hair, and my head fell back. He lightly bit down on my neck. I wanted to mount him then and there, but instead he pulled away.

I stared at him while he turned his back to stir the pasta. He switched off the burner and turned back around to see the confusion that I was sure was evident on my face.

"Mark." I wanted him, but more importantly I wanted him to want me. The way he kissed me, I could have sworn he felt something for me, but the way he could just let go made me wonder if maybe I was invading someone else's territory. He said he wasn't with Mary anymore, but he never said if he was with someone else, and I hadn't asked.

"Brook, we can't do this," Mark whispered, as if talking would shatter me.

"I understand," I murmured as a tear rolled down my face. I really didn't understand, but lying was better than hearing the words 'I don't want you' or even worse, 'I just don't feel that way about you.'

I climbed off the island and walked into my bedroom, then closed the door to put some distance between us. My heart was breaking. I cried into my pillow, wishing I could pull back my earlier admission. Wishing he didn't know how I felt. He was the one thing in my life I wanted but could never have.

It was already so late that by the time I dried my tears, I was getting up to shower for work. I needed to get adjusted to the office.

I climbed into the shower and began singing a song that lifted my spirits when I heard my bedroom door open. I quickly rinsed and grabbed the towel to exit. Mark was standing in the shower door when I pulled back the curtain.

I took a glance to see the effect my wet naked body was having on his pants, and felt a little better about the situation. He was standing there with a bowl of food and a fresh cup of coffee.

"I will get dressed and meet you in the kitchen. Give me about ten minutes."

Mark nodded and walked out of the bathroom. I quickly towel dried my hair and turned on my straightener. I applied my make-up, and then straightened my long black hair. I stared into the mirror and saw the dead girl staring back at me.

I shook it off and got dressed in a black pencil skirt with a silk lilac button-down shirt, placing my favorite black blazer on top. I put my crisscross strapped heels on, and made my way to my door.

Mark was sitting at the island. He turned to look my way as I stood in the doorway. I sat down on a stool, and Mark made me a new bowl of pasta since the other had grown cold.

"You should really get a few hours of sleep before you head into work." Mark's voice reverberated through me like a hot flash. I loved it when he spoke with that tone. I took a sip of coffee and bit into the pasta. It was as mouth-watering as Mark was.

"I am heading in to set up my office. I will be there through lunch. Then I plan to head back home and sleep."

We finished eating in silence. There were things to say, but I felt like we didn't need to bring it up. I was enjoying his comfort and his silence. Mark placed his hand over mine and I relished the feel of him even though I knew it was merely a tease.

"I want officers with you all day today," Mark whispered, low enough that I barely caught the words.

"I don't need it. I don't need the protection. No one even knows the case is mine yet."

There was a tension in the air that seemed to wrap around each of us and constrict our lungs and make life uncomfortable.

"You will accept it because it is non-negotiable. The last prosecutor died when we got our first real lead. That won't happen to you."

Mark was worried. I could understand where he was coming from, but that did not change the fact that no one knew I was on the case yet. I really didn't want to fight with him. I took a deep breath and exhaled slowly.

"Mark, I don't want strangers forced to give up their day to follow me around everywhere. If there is a threat against me, it is imaginary because no one has heard it yet."

Mark stood and walked to my front door. He unlocked it and opened it up. I watched as two men walked in. They were the same ones who had followed Mark into the park to get me earlier. They were both wearing running shoes with jeans and had on different t-shirts. Mark was speaking in a low voice so I could not understand what he was saying.

When he turned back, the look on his face had me rolling my eyes. He had already ordered people to follow me. I knew without him saying a word.

"Always have to do things your way, don't we?" I asked, as I walked into my bedroom and packed my laptop into my brown Dooney & Burke laptop bag. It didn't match my outfit, but I was not digging through the few unpacked boxes to see where my black bag was. I was livid that he would do this without even talking to me.

I walked to the door where I met the broad-shouldered, muscular men. This would be a perfect fantasy if I were one of those girls who drooled over firemen calendars. Normally I would be all over them, but as pissed as I was, they looked like they had just walked out of a children's television show—all innocent smiles and obvious good intentions.

"Brooklyn, this is Abbott and Costello," Mark replied with a smile aimed at the men.

I was annoyed that I wasn't even afforded the courtesy of being told their real names. Instead, they were given nicknames that matched actors who had been around long before their time.

In a moment of pure courage, I set my bag down and got Mark's attention. I unzipped my skirt and let it fall. All three were able to see my black lace underwear, but more importantly they could see the gun that rested in its holster on my upper thigh.

"I will be fine. Scout's honor." I held up three fingers and gave him a smug smile. I pulled my skirt up and tucked in my shirt before zipping it. Mark shook his head at me as I pushed past the men. It was nearly three in the morning, and anyone who approached me at this hour would be shot anyway.

My anger brewed during my elevator ride down. I exited the elevator in the lobby and saw the boy-toy security guards waiting for me. It irked me even further that they ran down all five floors without breaking a sweat. This was not going to be a good Monday.

CHAPTER
Five

THE FIRST WEEK AT MY new job passed in a blur. I did not even have the time to set up my office. I was spending all my time in the archives going over the last prosecutor's cases. There were appeals, and grand jury testimonies that were set up. I had not even been briefed on the cases. My boss had offered to divvy up the caseload until I caught up, but I wanted them to pile the work on. It would keep my mind busy so I wasn't waiting for the next victim.

There was no evidence on the body of the girl we had found. She was not listed as a missing person yet, but Mark and I would both continue to check daily. I tried not to think about it, but if we were going to catch the killer he would need to make a mistake with his next victim. I shuddered with fear and anxiety to think someone else would have to die for those women to get justice.

I saw Mark in the afternoons when he relieved my security for dinner. Those guys irked me, even though they were very good and blended into my surroundings. I didn't notice them, but it annoyed me to know they were somewhere babysitting me.

I packed up my work for the day and headed upstairs so I could go home. My dad had bailed on lunch as expected, but he was supposed to pick me up for dinner tonight. I wanted to get home and shower before he arrived.

I saw Mark standing outside his Escalade as I walked out of the building. He walked to my door and opened it for me. I piled my bags and the large box filled with case files into the backseat of his SUV and climbed in the front.

The gray leather interior was like a hot bath after a long day. Even though I didn't want to admit it, having Mark there to bring me home every day was a welcome relief. I kicked off my strappy heels and leaned back into the heated seat. The lumbar support was exactly what I needed after a week like this one.

Mark held my hand across the console the entire way home. He'd started doing it every day. I must have been tired because I remembered looking at him holding my hand, and the next thing I knew he was waking me up and we were across the river, in front of my apartment.

I yawned and Mark lifted me out of the SUV as though I was his bride. I snuggled into him and was quite content to stay against his chest when I heard a familiar voice.

"Put her down!"

"Nikolas, stop it," I shouted. "He was merely trying to help me." Mark slowly let my legs fall to catch my weight. As soon as I was standing between them, I knew this would not go well if I couldn't stop it.

"Aren't has-been mafia lords supposed to stay on the lower west side?" Mark asked as he stepped closer to Nikolas.

"If that were true, then shouldn't cops stay in Jersey where they *can* protect their own?" Nikolas countered, as he and Mark were nearly chest to chest.

I was too tired for any of this. I pushed between them and tried to shove them apart but only got my arm between them. Neither of them were going to budge.

"Nikolas, aren't we supposed to go to dinner?"

My dad looked my way and then back at Mark. It almost seemed like he growled as he turned to look at me again.

"Lyubov Moya, I hate that you are so tired that you need a Neanderthal to carry you inside. Maybe we should reschedule dinner."

I hated it when he called me his love in Russian. He only called me that when he wanted something. The fact that those words left my dad's lips was a sign that maybe dinner should be canceled. Then, something occurred to me.

"Mark is going to join us for dinner, aren't you, Mark?" I gave him a pleading stare. I even put my hands up like I was praying.

"Yes, I was going to escort her to dinner tonight. She is not to be left unattended until we catch this killer."

I breathed a sigh of relief when my dad made an excuse not to go to dinner. When he walked off, Mark and I gathered all my things from the SUV and carried them into the apartment.

Once inside, I set everything in the living room so I could spread out and work over the weekend. Mark stood speechless in my foyer like a bellhop waiting for a tip. I discarded my blazer and untucked my shirt as I walked toward him.

"I am going to pour some wine and watch reruns of the Big Bang Theory from my DVR. Do you want to join me?" I asked. I could see he wanted to say something, but he remained stoic. I turned around and noticed a new photo hanging on my wall. He must have seen it first.

There was an eleven by thirteen-inch black framed photo of a blue forget-me-not, with a white card tucked in the corner. When I reached for the envelope, Mark stopped me. He pulled his gun and began searching the apartment.

My anxiety should have been higher, but my curiosity was overriding every other emotion I could have conjured. After Mark cleared the apartment, he took tweezers from my bathroom and pulled the envelope from its spot. He placed it on the island and stared at me.

I went into the bathroom and retrieved gloves from a hair dye kit Kate had left behind. In the kitchen, I opened the envelope to find a small white card with calligraphy writing on the front in black. Mark and I read it over and over again in disbelief.

Hello Brooklyn,

I wanted to extend a cordial welcoming to the game that has begun. It took five victims to get you to come out and play. I wonder how many more will succumb to the game before you catch me. Remember as the game unfolds the fear you will feel is merely a myth. These women are not the one I want, they merely look like the one I want. Can't wait to have you all to myself.

I looked up at Mark in silence. I wanted him to tell me everything would be okay. I wanted him to say he would catch the bad guy. He said nothing. Instead, he gathered me into his arms and held me close. His chin rested atop my head while his comfort surrounded me.

Once I was a little more composed, I pulled back and stood up on my toes to plant a soft kiss on his cheek. Then I went to make coffee as he called for the crime scene crew to come and look for any evidence.

Within half an hour, my apartment was crawling with police and crime scene investigators. Even the coroner came out to see how I was doing since the police psychologist and chaplain were working with someone else at the moment.

"How are you, Ms. Montgomery?" James asked.

"I am stunned, but I am all right. How are you, Dr. Garie?"

"I was worried about you. It seems you are handling this better than I gave you credit for," James replied as he poured a cup of coffee.

"It's not that bad. Some insane serial killer broke into my apartment and left me a picture with a note telling me he wants me to play along." I spoke quietly, letting him know that I was perfectly capable of handling this.

"Ms. Montgomery, I think you are in denial about the severity of the situation. Please sit down." James indicated the small chairs along the table across from the island. I went with him to hear him out. "I am not a psychologist. I only did one psych rotation in medical school, but I think maybe you should be taking this seriously."

"Dr. Garie, I assure you I am taking this seriously. The answer is evident, don't you think?"

James tilted his head and studied me for a moment. It seemed he didn't understand what I was trying to say. The answer was crystal clear in my head. It was so simple.

"Dr. Garie, I merely have to exclude myself from the case," I whispered, to make sure no one else heard me.

"Ms. Montgomery, do you really think that is a good idea?"

"I don't want to, but it is clear what needs to happen. In the note, he says it took five victims to get me to come out and play. Therefore, he wanted me to be the one who would prosecute. Then he goes on to say 'before I catch him' instead of saying 'if I catch him.' If I walk away, he won't have the one thing he has been trying to get."

James nodded at the conclusion I had drawn. After a couple sips of coffee, his face looked stricken. He seemed to be pondering something that I was unaware of.

"Ms. Montgomery, if you excuse yourself from the case, wouldn't psychology dictate that he would kill more people to try to get you back? If he thinks of this as a game, then how do you forfeit the win against an unknown opponent in a game with no rules?"

I sat and thought about it for a moment. James was right. He probably would kill more women. He would act out in haste as things would no longer be going his way. It was a frightful thought that others who looked like me would die because I left, but murderers that act in haste make mistakes, and that was what we needed to find him and put him on death row.

I didn't want to talk about it anymore. I excused myself and walked into my bedroom. The walls were covered in fingerprint dust and my blankets had been taken into evidence. I was tired, and there were too many people around. I packed for a few days and then picked up the phone to book a room at the Marriott Marquis.

I brought out two black rolling suitcases. Tweedle Dum and Tweedle Dumber stared at me like I had a horn growing out of my forehead. I rolled my eyes as I walked ahead and parked the suitcases by the front door. Then I went and gathered up freshly dusted case files and put them back in the box.

"Brooklyn, what are you doing?" Mark asked from behind me.

"I am going to a hotel. I need this stuff to get some work done." I crawled around, gathering up more folders and placing them in the box. I felt hands on me before I was lifted off the floor. I was placed on my feet to face a very angry looking Mark.

"Why don't you stay with me?" he asked sternly.

"We both know why that would not work. I have a room at the Marriott. You can send my security guards over there to check out the hotel," I retorted. My patience was wearing thin in my exhaustion.

"Abbott and Costello will take you to the hotel and clear it. I want them in the room with you and a team outside the room until I get there. This is not up for debate. This is how things are going to happen," Mark growled. I was apparently pushing his buttons tonight, only I really didn't care at the moment. I just wanted some sleep.

"Fine, but I am taking the case files and my clothes." I glared at him and placed my hands on my hips for effect.

"No, not until the apartment is cleared. Nothing leaves. I will bring it to you when we are done here. Do not leave the hotel without telling your entire team where you are going so they can check it first."

I took a second to think about my attitude. Knowing the pressure he is under, I turned to apologize to Mark, but before I could say a word, I heard my name across the room and everyone froze. It was my boss. District Attorney Taylor Cross had bellowed my name, bringing everything to a halt.

"Ms. Montgomery, can I see you and Detective Stone outside in the hallway, please." It wasn't a question.

I felt Mark's hand on my back before I moved, and he led me into the hallway as the other officers went back to invading my privacy. I just wanted sleep, but it seemed no one else wanted the same thing.

"Give me one reason we don't let the FBI handle it from here." My boss glared at me. He was a handsome man with black hair. His tanned skin showed the Latin in his blood, but his green eyes contrasted it. He wasn't much older than me but gained his office through his parents' popularity. His father had become a judge of the Supreme Court, and his mother had been a trial lawyer until she passed away a few years back.

"Mr. Cross, I can give you a reason," I said. "He wanted me to chase him. I am not sure why he is fixated on me, but I have an idea. I think he might be an enemy of my father. No one else knows me, and the press release is not supposed to happen until Monday afternoon. No one knows my father's enemies better than Detective Stone here. At least give Mark a chance to look into it, and at the press release I will step down."

My boss glared at me, while Mark's hand rested on the small of my back. Mark hadn't said anything, but I felt like this was between my boss and myself.

"Ms. Montgomery, it is too late for press releases. A fake newspaper was put out on every newsstand and convenience store this afternoon. It has everything in it, including your visit to the crime scene last weekend. I was not even notified that you went down to thescene!"

Taylor growled at me as he handed me the paper

The front page read, *Mafia's iconic daughter starts new job at District Attorney's office by running from the latest Cut-Me-Not crime scene.* The article went on to state everything that had happened. I got about halfway down the article when the elevator to my floor opened and Kate came barreling out.

"Oh, thank God you're okay," she rambled, then hugged me and nearly crushed me in her arms.

"Why wouldn't I be all right?" I asked with confusion lacing my words.

She grabbed the paper and fumbled it a bit until it showed the bottom paragraph.

"The article. Right here under this paragraph, it says, 'Miss Montgomery is ready to play a round with the Cut-Me-Not killer and see if she can come out on top. Watch her apartment, folks. The blue lights from the NYPD will tell the tale of her fate.' Then I pulled up and there are blue lights everywhere. The coroner's van is even here."

Kate wept, and I held her. I saw my boss's face from over her shoulder. He was looking at Mark and it was clear there was an unease that everyone was sensing, but no one was saying anything.

"Brooklyn, rather than encroach on your privacy, I am going to put everything out there," my boss said. "Your apartment is compromised. You cannot stay here. The killer has named a target and it is people who look like you because for some reason he wants to play a game with you. I think you have a more than professional relationship with Detective Stone, but I don't want to know if it is true. I want you to think about this before you step down. I came to all these conclusions in the ten minutes or so I have been here. The outside world is watching you. The killer is watching you. Do you want him to see you running from him, or do you want him to see that you can fight back?"

I took a deep breath. I never thought about what people saw when they looked at me. I am quick to judge a person by what they are wearing, how they look, what their disposition is like, and even how they interact with others. It is a nasty little habit I picked up when I started dating. It has kept me safe, but there was no way to know what others concluded about me.

My brain started spinning. Would he attack Mark because of the way we appeared? Is his interest in me romantic? Would he hurt Kate? Is he already close to me? What has he seen?

My stomach ached and my heart raced. I felt Mark's hand leave the small of my back and wrap around my waist. Mark and Taylor were talking to each other and Kate was peeking into my apartment to see the people scurry through my things. Everything sounded muffled behind the loud beats of my heart that were overtaking my eardrums.

I tightened my stance to ensure my standing position as my heart raced and my head felt weightless. As my breaths shortened, I felt weak and dizzy. I tried to calm myself down, but my body refused to allow it. Everything turned to a hazy gray when I heard people shouting my name. Then silence, and everything went dark.

CHAPTER
Six

I HEARD SOFT VOICES WHISPERING around me. My heart rate slowed. My breaths were even and regulated. I moved my arms to discover I had a blanket on top of me. Opening one eyelid, I saw that I was inside my hotel room.

The light was on in the dining room, which was right outside the bedroom. I saw Doctor Garie, the coroner, talking to Abbott and Costello, my security team. They were speaking so quietly I could not make out what they were saying.

I was exhausted, unsure of how I wound up in the hotel room. I would rather sleep than get answers. I rolled on my side and into a familiar male chest. I snuggled up against him and wrapped the blanket around me tightly.

Mark was under the blanket facing me. He wrapped his arm around me and tugged me close. His lips pressed against my forehead, and I immediately felt as though everything would turn out all right. No matter what we faced, at the end of the day we could depend on each other.

I always believed I would lose Mark to Mary. I thought he would marry her, and then I would never be able to stand seeing them happy together. I thought he would eventually find a new best friend, leaving me behind.

"How do you feel?" Mark whispered. With both arms around me, he held me close. My head rested on his shoulder and faced his chest. I breathed in his manly scent. It was an intoxicating aroma that made my mouth water.

"I am good as long as you're here," I murmured. The entire week dissipated and became a distant memory while he cradled me in his arms. I knew he did not feel the same way about me, but his presence was comforting.

"You scared me," Mark said, pulling back so I had to look at him. "Don't ever do that to me again."

"Detective Stone," a voice called out from behind closed doors. "Is she awake, yet? Would you like me to check her over?" the voice said. I knew it was Dr. Garie, but I ignored his words and made no move to speak to anyone.

"No, please get some rest yourself. Have Abbott and Costello take a break, and let the guards outside know she is fine with me. Everyone needs to rest and we will start digging through what we have with fresh eyes in the morning." Mark's chest vibrated with the authority in his tone. I heard the double doors shut and a few moments later I heard the men leaving.

Silence descended, and I was no longer tired. I didn't want to talk or move, I just wanted to stay next to Mark. I lined my body up with his and wiggled here and there to get the position I wanted.

"You have to stop grinding against me."

I froze and waited for him to say something else. When he didn't, I went back to trying to get comfortable. I draped my leg across the top of his and brought his thigh in between my legs.

"Mark," I whispered as I leaned up to see his face. He was looking down at me while his head rested on the pillow. I had a sudden urge to confess my feelings all over again, but it wouldn't help either of us. I did, however, need him to know that he couldn't be a hero for me.

"If something happened to you because of me—"

Mark stopped my words by flipping me onto my back and climbing on top of me. I inhaled sharply and tried to finish my sentence, but he leaned down and placed his mouth against mine. Those soft velvety lips had me yearning for the one thing I couldn't have.

Suddenly it all came to light. I pushed Mark back and sat up. I climbed out of the bed, discovering I was in my pajamas. That was a conversation I would be having when my brain slowed down.

I opened the door and went to the box of case files. Mark followed me, with an intense gaze on his face that I couldn't remember ever seeing before. I started opening files and tossing them into a chaotic mess on the table. Red, blue, yellow, green. The folders made a rainbow as the pile grew higher, and then there was the one powder blue file. It matched the color of the forget-me-not flowers that were left at the crime scene.

I opened it to reveal the threats the previous Assistant District Attorney had received.

I hadn't had time to read all of them, but I remembered one in which he mentioned wanting the one thing he couldn't have. The pages had the same handwriting as the note in my apartment. I sorted through them to find the one I needed. Then I handed it to Mark.

* No one will give me what I want. You won't walk away, continuing to play the game you were not invited to. If you continue to play, I will make you part of the game.

There is one thing I want and she is like a sunset over Brooklyn. Her hair is dark as night and eyes as blue as the ocean. Bring her to play and you may live to see another day.

Mark read it and then dropped the page on the ground, staring at me. He looked angry. I took a few steps back until I was against the window that overlooked a view of Times Square. He continued to bear down on me as though I was his prey.

"Mark," I whispered as my nerves ran amuck. Butterflies had taken root in my stomach. My palms grew sweaty, my thighs moistened and my mouth became dry.

"Shh," Mark whispered, as his finger covered my lips. Then he replaced it with his mouth. I stood motionless as he kissed me. Unaware of what was happening, but wanting so much more. My heart was breaking even as I fell deeper in love with Mark.

I opened to him, and he pressed his body against mine, inhaling the moan that left my lips. All five of my senses were being overloaded by him. I could no longer hear anything but the rapid beating of my heart. I tasted coffee and whipped cream on his tongue as I inhaled his manly sandalwood scent. I looked into his eyes when he pulled away. My body burned with the need to touch him everywhere.

"Tell me no," Mark whispered as he dropped to his knees. I watched in fascination while he untied the bow on my drawstring shorts. I shivered as I watched him pull down my shorts, exposing a pair of black lace underwear.

I was already panting and clinging to the glass and he had barely touched me. He placed a kiss on my stomach just above my underwear and I thought my body was on fire. I watched eagerly as he feathered kisses all around my underwear. He even pried my legs apart to kiss the inside of my thigh. I let out a groan as moisture flooded my thighs behind each kiss.

"Tell me to stop," he said, even as he tugged on my underwear. I refused to say a word or even whimper as he lowered them ever so slowly. I bit my lip to keep my sounds at a minimum. Despite my desire, I guarded my heart.

As my underwear reached the floor, he lifted my right leg and placed it over his shoulder. I nearly lost my balance as he did the same to the left. Then he stood up with my legs draped over his shoulders and my body six feet up in the air. My back to the open window facing Times Square, and my pussy facing a very hungry Mark.

I had nowhere to go and nothing to grab onto except for him. I grabbed my breasts instead of pushing him into me. As ready as I was to come, I would surely suffocate him. I watched his face below me, facing my entrance, and felt the blood rush to my clit as it throbbed with each breath he exhaled.

"Last chance. Tell me you don't want me." Mark looked up, waiting for my words.

"I love you, Mark," I murmured breathlessly, and then I pushed his head into my crotch. I heard a light laugh, but the sound didn't last long as I felt that first brush of his tongue. I twisted my hands in his silky hair and moaned with pleasure.

I released his hair and pulled my tank top down to expose my breasts. I tugged on the nipples as Mark rode me higher and higher up the cliff. My racing heart had finally drowned out my moans. I needed this release more than my next breath.

"Please." I gasped between moans. His pace quickened and suddenly I felt it coming on strong. I tightened my stomach and my thighs. Wanting to scratch and claw up the glass window, I was forced to endure every unrelenting lick and thrust. I bit my lip and pinched my breasts as I screamed through the beginning of my orgasm. Electricity pulsated as the waves crashed over me. As he continued, his onslaught of my clit heat ravaged my body. Sweat dripped from my brow as I was steamrolled beneath the agonizing pleasure he bestowed upon me.

I struggled to catch my breath as he lowered me. I was grateful he kept a hold on me because I didn't think I could stand. My legs trembled. He slanted his head and placed his mouth over mine. I tasted myself on him and it only stirred the pulse behind my clit once more.

Mark ripped my tank top off and I stood completely naked before him. The glass at my back was soothing as my skin flamed while he looked over my body. Then he turned me to face the glass. I could see all the lights in Times Square, and the people walking down below. We were so high up that they looked tiny.

I heard the clasp of a belt and went to turn around and help him when he grabbed my hands and placed them palm down against the glass. Then he whispered in my ear.

"Don't move or tell me to go away."

I said nothing and waited. I felt his breath on my neck and his body against my back as I heard the foil package opening behind me. The sound of him removing his jeans caused me to startle, and his hands rubbed on my back to soothe me.

I spread my legs, and Mark trailed his finger down, probing inside my entrance.

"You are so ready for me, Brook," he said with a grunt of appreciation.

"Always," I replied as his large head probed my entrance.

As he slid his cock inside me, I gasped and held my breath. I was swollen from my orgasm and it made everything tighter. I felt as though he commanded my body with his long hard shaft, and I was his for the taking. He was so long that I felt at any second I would be lifted off my feet by his manhood. As he reached the hilt, he lifted my left leg and held it at the knee. Then did the same with the other. I was spread open, facing the glass with my knees up as my feet hung in the air.

I had never felt anyone so deep inside me before. There was a bite of pain and a mountain of pleasure. I could feel my walls constrict around him in a melody that matched my heartbeat. I placed my forehead on the cool glass and slowly began breathing again.

Mark pulled in and out of me as if he was leading an orchestra. Everything was done in a rhythm that took him where he wanted to go. From this position, the head of his cock was grazing that rough patch inside me that made my body scream out for more.

"Look at the people down there," Mark murmured as he kissed my neck. I turned my head to give him more room. "Imagine they all see us. They all see that you are here with me. They see that it is *my* cock you crave and it will be *my* name you scream. No one else can have you if you are here with me."

I was so close to climaxing again, but his words broke my heart. I wanted this so badly that I couldn't see it for what it was. He was marking his territory by being inside me. It wasn't about love or anything even close to that. I felt like the tree a dog would piss on. It would go around and around, marking the spot, but at the end of the day no one loved the tree. The dog just wanted to make it clear he was the alpha.

I don't know how, but I could feel my impending orgasm as a tear rolled down my cheek. My heart was all in and thankfully Mark couldn't see that. As he sped up his rhythm, I closed my eyes and memorized every sound and breath he took. I reveled in every grunt and groan. I would dream about the sounds heard when my moans clashed with his as we both found ecstasy with each other.

I screamed as the orgasm tore through my body and shattered my heart. Pleasure and pain wracked my entire being. I slapped the glass and tightened down on him. He continued to drive into me, riding me down from my orgasm. Mark pumped into me two more times and grit his teeth as he came.

He lowered his head onto my shoulder and released my legs slowly as he caught his breath.

When he pulled out, I immediately missed him. I wanted to pull him back inside me. I wanted him to put a band-aid over my aching heart to make it all better, but I was a grown woman and this was not how life worked. When he backed up, I took a quick swipe at my tears and turned to face him. I could see in the mirror across from me my skin had flushed crimson from its normal alabaster color.

I forbid myself a glance at his manhood. I knew it was wrapped in a condom, but curiosity had always been one of my vices. My heart called out that we'd made love, while my brain told me I was stupid and reminded me he was not as invested as I was. This was a friendship that had gone too far tonight.

I grabbed my clothes and headed for the shower. I couldn't even bring myself to look Mark in the eye in case he saw how shattered I was.

I turned on the shower and climbed inside before it was even warm. The tears fell down my cheeks and into the drain. It wasn't a moment later that the shower door was being opened and a naked Mark walked inside. I moved so he could get under the water as well, but he didn't step forward.

"Brooklyn," Mark said.

I placed my head in the water so he couldn't see my face. It was bad enough I had confessed how I felt and even gave myself to him and all I got in return was a couple of devastating orgasms and a broken heart.

I couldn't think of anything to say, but it didn't matter. The problem of sleeping with your best friend is they know what is beneath the surface. Mark enveloped me into his arms and I cried on him until the water ran cold.

Then he turned off the shower and placed a towel around me. He led me out of the shower where he donned a white robe, and carried me in my towel to the bed. He laid me down and covered me up, then crawled in beside me. I curled into him and prayed for sleep, but it wouldn't come soon enough.

"Brooklyn, I do care about you," Mark whispered as I laid my head on his chest.

"Don't. You'll only make it worse." I had enough going on to fill up my BS meter and I didn't need him in that mix.

"Brook, please hear me out."

I turned away from him, but he didn't allow any distance between us. I kept my back to his chest for the rest of the night. Neither of us said another word to each other, and we didn't sleep until the sun began to rise. Mark held me and gave me the comfort I always seemed to need when he was around, and he stayed right by my side the entire time.

CHAPTER
Seven

I SLEPT ABOUT AN HOUR AND my brain woke me up with thoughts of where my relationship with Mark was headed. I lifted his arm and slid out of bed. I thought I had gotten away unscathed, but then I heard Mark's voice as I reached the door.

"Where are you going?" He sounded gruff. I turned to look at him and smiled the best I could without giving away my intentions.

"I am going to shower and make coffee. Sleep a little longer. It is going to be a long day."

Then I walked out of the bedroom, closing the doors behind me. After brewing a pot of coffee, I turned on the shower but made no move to get in.

I walked to the front door in nothing but my towel and asked the police officers who were stationed there to run and get breakfast for themselves. I gave them a little wink to make them think Mark and I were about to have sex, and watched as they got into the elevator.

I grabbed my bag and put on a pair of skinny jeans and my gray knee high boots. Then I dressed in a white tank top and a gray sweater that hung off my shoulder. I quickly brushed out my hair and applied my make-up. A quick spray of my perfume, and I was almost ready.

I clipped my holster to my black belt, double-checking my gun was loaded. Then I settled her in the holster. I threw everything into my bag and rolled it out the front door.

As I entered the lobby, I begged the concierge to hold my bag until I figured out what it was I was doing. He agreed, but must have known who I was because he was calling my room as soon I walked off. Mark would be furious, but I needed space. I needed time to think.

I grabbed a cab and headed toward the Empire State Building. Nothing says distance like being one hundred and two stories up in the air. I just needed a little time to clear my head.

I surrendered my gun with complaint as security wouldn't let me up with it. My badge did nothing for me here. The trip up in the elevator was numbing. I felt constricted and worried what would happen if I was found. Mark would be livid. My boss would be furious. My dad would become a saint compared to the wrath of Mark and Taylor.

Upon leaving the elevator on the eighty-sixth floor, I stared at the view in front of me. I was shaken when I felt my phone vibrate in my purse, then opened it to see a very angry text from Mark and nineteen missed calls.

There was a little boy standing with his mother enjoying the view as the sun rose over New York City. I watched as he played with his teddy bear, unaware of the danger lurking in the city. He was safe as long as he didn't have anything that resembled me, after all the killer only wanted women who looked like me. Then he looked at me, his bright blue eyes glimmering, and I nearly vomited with the thought that he could one day be a victim merely because his eyes matched mine.

I downloaded a game to my phone and turned it on airplane mode, then I tip-toed over and handed it to him.

"This is our secret," I whispered, while his mother looked through the viewfinder. He immediately sat down by her feet and began playing without saying a word. I walked back inside and took the elevator to floor one hundred and two.

As I stared out the windows, the storm in the distance kept me mesmerized. I watched the lighting jump, placing my hands on the glass and looking downward. It was so surreal, my brain was playing flashbacks of being against the glass the previous night.

My nipples hardened and my heart raced. My body was betraying my heart. I could still feel every touch and kiss. I yearned for him to be with me, but my heart begged me to make him stay away. I didn't even hear the man's voice until he placed a hand on my shoulder.

"Ma'am, are you all right?" he asked.

I startled, then turned to find a very tall security guard behind me. He was broad shouldered, and something about his demeanor made him seem like a country boy. He had dirty blond hair and familiar green eyes.

My stomach quivered with unease. I knew his eyes from the man in the park, but nothing else about him made him seem like the same man.

"I am okay, just needed some air," I replied, hoping he would understand the implication that I needed some space. He did not get the hint. Instead, he stood beside me, looking down on the buildings below.

"I have always been told I am a great listener. Anything you need to get off your chest?" he asked.

"I don't know you. Why would I tell you?" I replied hastily.

"Ma'am, you would be surprised what people have told me, when they come up here, and look at the world the way you are looking at it right now. You are standing against the glass as if you wish you could fall."

I took a step back and turned toward him, placing my hands on my hips.

"I am not suicidal. I am working. I just needed some air, and furthermore, I just had my heart broken, which is why I needed to get some fresh air *alone*."

"I meant no harm, ma'am." He lifted his hands in a defensive manner. Then, as he lowered his hands, he asked, "What did he do?"

"He didn't love me," I replied, a tear rolling down my face. I turned back to the glass and faced the storm. I knew how it felt. So full of life and energy, but after a few raindrops it would feel weak and dissipate into the atmosphere.

"Ma'am, I don't know you or your story, but I can tell you what my momma always said. When someone breaks your heart, you coin toss. Heads, you give them one last chance. Tails, you forget they even existed. I have a coin, do you want to play a *game* with me?"

I immediately turned and out of instinct I reached to pop the strap on my holster that I had surrendered before coming up in the elevator. I stared at him, watching as he flipped the coin and waited for my response.

"Games are for children," I retorted. "This is real life." I backed away from him as he smiled like a Cheshire cat, and I suddenly missed my phone. It was him, I knew it was. I walked back through the doors as he followed me.

"You really are a beautiful woman," he said. "I love the way your hair accents your eyes. Whoever he was doesn't deserve you. Maybe he should have his heart ripped out."

I swallowed hard as the elevator took its time rising to the top to get me. My palms grew sweaty as he came closer to me.

"You stay away from him," I said firmly. "If it came to a choice, I would lay down my life for him. Under no circumstances should it be the other way around."

He had not even admitted that he had done anything; he merely implied things that made me uncomfortable. I was alone and defenseless.

"I am not in the habit of ripping out hearts, ma'am."

The elevator grew louder, and I knew it would be there momentarily. This was the do or die moment people talk about. They say it is either fight or flight, but they forget the third option—freeze. When facing an intense situation, people either fight, run, or they freeze. I was frozen.

He reached into his pocket and my body began to tremble with anxiety. He pulled something out, very slowly. The elevator door opened and the little boy with my phone walked out with his mother. They walked between me and the security guard, and I backed into the elevator as the security guard smiled. The doors began to close, and he threw something inside.

I looked to the floor to see what it was. There were tons of dead-headed blue forget-me-nots. I fell to the floor and let the adrenaline run through me. My body was shaking so much that I had no control.

When I arrived on the eighty-sixth floor, I glanced up to see Mark and a dozen police officers waiting. Mark scooped me up in his arms and held me as the adrenaline coursed through me fiercely.

"Are you all right?" he asked, noticing the flowers on the floor. I nodded, but words wouldn't come.

Mark took me onto a secondary elevator after shouting orders. He set me down inside, and looked me over. Something on my face must have given me away. Because he asked the attendant to step out and then we were alone as the door closed.

Mark's expression changed from concern to anger in a split second after he saw I was all right. I pushed him against the elevator and grabbed his face. I pulled his lips to mine. As his tongue dove into my mouth, his flavor hit me and sent me reeling for more.

I grabbed his belt and loosened it as he pushed the emergency stop button. He pressed me against the elevator wall and unbuttoned my pants, pulling them down. When I couldn't take it anymore, he unzipped my knee-high boots. I pulled him back up to me with one boot on and one boot off. My jeans matched with one leg on and one leg off.

I unzipped his pants and dove my hand inside while my other hand worked to free his cock. I dropped to my knees as his pants fell. He moved to the back wall and gripped the railing as I sucked the head of his cock into my mouth.

The large purple head appeared as angry as the rest of him. I licked him from balls to head and looked up. His eyes were dilated, his breathing rushed. He no longer looked angry. He placed his hand on the back of my head and showed me the rhythm he liked as I flattened my tongue and took him to my throat.

I took my time in tasting him, using my hand to follow my mouth as he was too long to get him all the way inside. I tightened my grip and he released my hair to hold the rail.

I tasted the pre-cum and wanted to give him more. I tremored with my own need until he vibrated right out of my mouth. I continued to pump him, but he must have felt as I did.

He pulled me off of him and lifted me to my feet in one swift move. He spread my legs, pushed my panties aside and immediately pushed his hardened cock inside me. The initial stretch burned and had me gasping for breath. I gripped his shoulders. I needed this, and I needed him.

"Condom." He gritted his teeth as he spoke. I didn't want him to pull out of me.

"Pill," I whispered, as I grabbed his head to bring his mouth over mine. He picked me up and took the few steps to the wall and placed me against it. He pushed in and out of me as he kissed my neck. I moaned in his ear as I clawed at his shirt.

This was what I needed at the moment. He rode me hard and fast. I didn't see my orgasm coming until it was upon me. It was intense. My body bowed against the wall and forced him farther inside me. The bite of pain from it sent me spiraling to the heavens and cresting before collapsing on his shoulder as he drove me down the cliff.

I felt the stirring in my stomach and swore it couldn't be true. One orgasm was all I ever managed vaginally, but here it was, coming on me fast. I squirmed trying to escape the impending orgasm that would steal my soul, but it was too late. I bit down on his shoulder to keep my screams down as I hit and slapped at him when it peaked and sent me over the edge.

He rode me down my orgasm, whispering something I couldn't understand. My heart roared with energy as it tried to beat out of my chest. My adrenaline rush exited in my orgasm and I was suddenly very tired. Mark pumped into me a few more times before throwing his head back and gritting his teeth. His orgasm had him leaning his head on the cool wall and looking down into my eyes.

He lowered me and we both got dressed. My legs were once again like jelly and I struggled with staying upright. The lack of sleep and parade of emotions had me crashing to the floor in pure exhaustion. Mark started the elevator again and helped me get dressed during our descent.

"Brooklyn, want to tell me what happened here?" Mark asked as he helped me get my boot back on.

"I needed some air, and there was a man here. He was dressed as a guard, but the things he said made me think it was him."

Mark helped me to my feet and kept an arm around me as he inspected me.

"We will talk about this, Brooklyn." He waved at the air around us. "You have put me off or run away each time I try. Now after you explain the flowers we are going to have a cup of coffee and you and I will discuss this thing that is happening between us."

"Mark, I can't handle hearing the words come out of your mouth that you don't want me. Put it off a few more days or a week, please."

He seemed to ignore me and snapped the holster shut on my pants.

"I can't keep passing work onto others so I can soothe you. I left work when you got nauseous, and here I am again helping you cascade down an adrenaline mountain. I need to be able to focus and I can't when you look at me the way you do."

"How do I keep looking at you?" I ask in a whisper, unable to meet his eyes.

"You stare at me with those deep blue eyes, and I can see you love me. Your full pouty lips beg me to kiss them. Your voice quivers when you get excited, which is the same thing it does when I am deep inside you. Your skin flourishes to life when I touch you. Everything about you pulls me in so fast that I have to run the opposite direction just to catch my breath."

I decided it was time to get off the subject. I knew if he went into any further detail someone would end up hurt and it would most likely be me. I wonder how he came to be here when I was here.

"How did you find me?" I asked softly.

"Your phone has its GPS on."

"Who ratted me out?" I asked, trying to hide the guilt that followed. I knew someone was in trouble for my actions.

"The cops you sent for breakfast have been relieved of duty pending an investigation."

There was the guilt. It came up and slapped me in the face. I never meant for anyone to get into that much trouble. I just wanted five minutes of freedom.

"This was my fault, not theirs. Tell me how to help them." I pleaded with the friend in Mark, hoping the detective in him didn't have any control in this.

"You helped them by getting them suspended. They both knew better than to take orders from anyone except their direct supervisor."

Another wave of guilt pierced my stomach and I felt sick. I was thinking about myself and my feelings, using others for my own gain without considering the impact it would have on their families. I would have to make it a point to have Mark take me over to their houses to apologize.

"Brooklyn, where did the flowers come from?" Mark asked, pulling me back from my own thoughts.

"He threw them in the elevator." I yawned.

"Was he wearing gloves?" Mark asked in an urgent rush.

"No, I don't think so." I remembered his hands from the coin but could not place if he was wearing gloves or not. I yawned again. I didn't think coffee would help at this point. I was so exhausted.

"Brooklyn, I am going to drop you off at the hotel and get you into bed."

My eyebrows raised on that statement.

"Not for that, although I would never say no to that. What I mean is..."

I was finding humor in the way he tripped over his words because he was worried how I would take them.

"Brooklyn, you need to get some sleep. I need to go and see if they found anything. Hopefully, he left a print for us to follow. I am putting more officers in and outside your room. One will come and take your statement and one will come to get a description. I will call you and we will do dinner and talk."

I realized I had not told him about my phone, and looked down at my feet.

"What?" Mark asked.

"I gave my phone to a little kid when you wouldn't stop calling."

Mark laughed a little. I don't know what was so humorous, but something I had done was funny.

"What?" I asked.

"If he tracked you here the same way we did, he will be tracking a little kid for a while."

My face fell as I thought about what that might mean for the little kid's fate. I had never seen the guy before, so thinking he might be related to my dad's organization might have been wrong. I wanted to find him and stop him before he hurt someone's child.

"Brooklyn, I will call Kate and she will bring you a temporary phone. We can work it out while you get some sleep. No reason to look so down," Mark said as we neared the bottom floor.

"The kid had my eyes," I murmured, and Mark's face fell. He had the same thought I did.

He pulled out his phone and shouted orders into it to track my phone and get it from the child. I had turned on airplane mode, so maybe it wouldn't be traceable anymore. Every horrendous thought that could have entered my mind did at that moment.

Upon exiting the building, I saw Mark's Escalade parked out front with the police lights flashing in the front and back. I piled into the passenger seat and waited as he made what seemed like a hundred phone calls. He was so invested in this case. I would have to set aside my broken heart and feelings for Mark, or I would have to step down and let him work with someone else.

It wouldn't be fair to continue torturing myself with little sexual escapades that made me fall deeper in love with him. I couldn't continue to show him how much it hurt that he didn't see me that way. We needed to be able to hit a rewind button and go back to before I had ever admitted anything.

By the time we arrived at the hotel, the place was swarming with officers. They were not all in uniform, but the plainclothes detectives were carrying themselves in a demeanor I commonly saw in Mark. My boss was there, talking to Mark.

The next events flew by in a blur of exhaustion. One officer drew the suspect, another officer took a statement, and even my boss had a few choice words for my behavior, but he still would not let me step down. I climbed in the bed and drifted fast asleep while my boss was lecturing me.

CHAPTER
Eight

DREAMING

D ARKNESS WAS ALL AROUND ME. *Back in the same eerie hallway looking for the red door. I knew what would happen if I didn't get to the red door, because it had all happened before.*

Click clack—my heels were making the noise across the white marble floors. Walking through the darkness to find a door, my anxiety levels rose with each step.

Five doors down in the hallway, I heard a groan. Looking around to determine where the sound came from, I realized I could not go back. The floor and hallway behind me had disappeared. If I were to step back, I would fall into the darkness.

"Brook."

I heard someone call out my name in the dark. It was a man, and there was a pained groan.

"Who's there?" I called out. Taking a few steps forward, I heard the voice again.

"Brook."

I didn't want to go through any of the mahogany doors. I was confident those doors would take me back to meet the devil himself.

I started running, trying to find the familiar voice in the darkness.

"Brook," the voice called out again, this time with a cough as if gasping for air to breathe.

"Where are you?" I screamed back. Do I dare to open one of the mahogany doors?

Click clack, click clack—I froze. Those were not my heels on the floor making that noise. Panic escaped my lips with a shivered attempt to hold my breath. This couldn't be happening again. I listened for the groan and did my best to tune out the sounds of feet coming near.

The man's groan made him sound as if he were in absolute agony. Please, I silently begged to God or the universe. Whoever kept bringing me back to this place was showing little mercy. I had a choice as the footsteps grew closer. I could run and leave the man behind, or find him and risk going back to the one hundred and eighty-seventh floor.

I could never turn my back on someone. It wasn't in my DNA; I couldn't live with myself knowing I could have done something to help and refused. There was no way I would leave this man behind. I just needed to find him and get the hell out of there.

I heard the voice again. I had run too far as the voice was groaning behind me now. Fear took hold, as I made an instinctive decision to turn back. The non-

existent floor in the darkness seemed to return as I stepped to go back the way I'd come. When the floor returned, it was no longer the pretty white marble floor. The floor was blood red and the walls had turned to a burnt orange color. The doors had turned black in protest. It was the most horrible color array I had ever seen. Regardless of the difference, I knew what I had to do. I went from door to door, calling out.

I didn't dare turn the knobs. Keeping my hand on a knob, I heard the groan from behind the door. The voice was begging for me to come to him. Then out of the corner of my eye in the darkness, a shadowy figure moved. The shadow slowed as it neared, the clicking of the heels slowing as well. This shadow had been what was chasing me.

Emerging from the darkness was the woman I had tried to save before. She was wearing the same clothing. I recognized her green eyes and long blond hair. It was a relief, as I was no longer afraid. Instead, I was overwhelmed with sorrow for this woman. I kept my hand on the knob while the woman began to walk past me.

"Brookie, where are you?" The man's voice called out.

The pained groan said he was right behind the door. The woman stopped and turned back.

"Come save me, Brooklyn."

I was torn. I knew the man behind the door was strained for my help, but I also knew this woman needed me as well.

"Stay here with me," I implored her. A small smile slid across her face.

"Only you can save me," the woman said.

"Please, stay here with me. Let me help you." At this point, I was begging.

"Brookie, come back to me," the man's voice called out. I suddenly felt torn in two.

I wanted to run to the voice behind the door to seek safety. And I wanted to stay and help this woman.

Though the cost was high, I felt responsible for not stopping the devil the first time. Facing reality and being a grown-up sucked. I would have paid for someone else to choose which decision was right. Maybe I could save her and help him.

The blond woman looked over her shoulder as her body shuddered with fear. A large creature came walking out of the darkness. It was him. He wasn't a dragon this time. Instead, he had taken the shape of a lion.

One tilt of the head said he knew I was there. Even with that knowledge, he didn't alter his course as he slinked near us. Without a second thought, I put myself between him and the blond.

His golden mane was flawless. He was beautiful yet dangerous, and his predatory face and eyes of coal never blinked from the target. I tightened my grip on the doorknob, holding my other arm up to keep the blond behind me.

I was preparing myself for the fight of my life when I heard the man's voice from behind the door.

"Brookie, please come back to me. I can't live without you. Please."

I heard the terror in the voice behind the door but stood paralyzed in front of this creature which seemed to be growing larger with each step.

As he came upon me, he crouched down. I held my breath as I took a moment to swallow my fears and study him. He looked like a lion, but when I viewed him from the side, I noticed the skulls that made him into a dragon earlier were now in his stomach. In this shape, the souls were floating around as if they were screaming to get out. I was able to make out several faces from the case we had been working on.

My hand tightened on the doorknob as I heard the man sobbing. Still begging me to come through the door. I decided I would probably be safer if I walked away from the woman. But how could I walk away from someone in need?

The man's voice behind the door had a calming effect on me even in the face of the devil himself. As soothing as the voice was, it wasn't helping me find a way out of the situation.

What would stop the lion from coming through that door with us? He was enormous and could do and be whatever he wanted. I wanted to save at least one person if I could. I turned the knob quietly behind me. The lion laughed again.

"You shouldn't run from me," he warned. "But I do enjoy this game of chasing you." He spoke as if he knew what I was thinking.

I listened to the man's voice behind the door begging me to come back to him. The voice gave me confidence despite the situation I was in.

In one quick move, I opened the door and flung myself back, pulling the blond with me. The lion grabbed her right leg and began pulling her out into the hallway. I held her hands and tried to pull her back. The lion was strong and dragged us both back into the hallway. The blond was screaming, and I was fighting to hold onto to her with everything I had. She let go of my hands, and I could no longer hold her as she went flying out toward the lion. Sounds of screaming pierced the air as if the walls couldn't take the noise and bounced it around until it was absorbed by my ears. It was too late for her, and she was being ripped apart.

Instincts kicked in and I got to my feet and lunged toward the door to shut him out. Once the door was shut, I slumped down behind it and cried into my hands. I had to apply extra force, planting my feet so my body was against the door, hoping it would keep him out. After I composed myself and heard nothing but silence for a few minutes, I went looking for the male voice.

"Mark," I called out.

"I'm here, Brookie," he called back. I walked all around the room. There was nothing but darkness and the elevator. Refusing to get in the elevator, I did laps looking for him. The door flew open and there was the demon himself in the shape of a lion.

"I've waited long enough for you to play along. You are mine," he said in a predatory voice. He began to move toward me, taunting me to run.

"Mark, help me, please," I called out. As the lion grew closer, he swiped his claws at me and missed but it caused me to fall and hit my head.

"Brook, open your eyes," Mark called back. The demon moved in for the kill, standing over me.

It was too late. I couldn't help anyone. I failed to save anyone, even myself. I whispered, I'm sorry and I love you as the giant paw came down and cut me to shreds.

"WAKE UP, BROOKLYN!" A VOICE called out. I felt something touch me and went flying into defensive mode. I started swinging before I realized I was in the hotel room hitting my boss. Oh hell, this wouldn't end well.

"I'm sorry." I immediately started apologizing as my heart rate slowed and the air chilled the sweat that was dripping off me.

My boss didn't say anything so I got up and walked out of the bedroom, staring down the five officers who were talking amongst themselves. In the bathroom, I splashed cold water on my face. These dreams only happened every once in a while, but it seemed they were trying to tell me something.

I walked back out to see pity on the faces of the officers. I looked down my body and saw I was still wearing my sweater and jeans. I must have screamed in my sleep or something. They all looked like they felt sorry for me.

I walked into my bedroom to see my boss already had ice on the side of his eye.

"I am so sorry, sir. I was having a bad dream and thought you were going to eat me."

Taylor laughed as the words left my mouth. I'm sure I sounded odd, and I think I might've been bordering on sexual harassment just by saying it.

"I have been accused of many things, Ms. Montgomery, but I have never been punched in the head for wanting to eat someone." Taylor winked.

Relief washed over me that he was not as angry as I thought he would be. I laughed with him and allowed the humiliation I was feeling run its course.

"What are you doing here?" I asked.

"They found a lead. We came across a fingerprint. It gave us an eight-point match to a criminal. I already pulled a warrant, and Detective Stone is leading SWAT out to intercept the suspect and bring him in for questioning. I brought some photos of him I would like you to look at."

I released the breath I had been holding since he said Mark was leading SWAT. Those guys knew what they were doing, but it didn't stop the unease I felt about the entire situation.

I kept thinking nothing bad could happen because too much had been left unsaid. Mark and I still had to get our friendship back to what it should have been all along.

I watched as Taylor pulled out a file out of a briefcase that was sitting beside the bed. Another *powder blue folder with the words Cut-Me-Not written across the tab. My hands shook as I took it from him.*

I opened it and read the previous reports. Arson, murder, rape, distribution, and even assaulting an officer with evading arrest. This guy had been charged with a whole list of things but had never spent more than a few hours in jail. It didn't seem right.

I detested people like him. They committed heinous acts and never had to pay the penalty. Even when our system couldn't put the needle of death in their arm, I expected karma to handle it; but most days, it seemed like karma forgot the ones who needed to be dealt with the most.

I scrolled through the statements from the victims. It seemed like him when I came to the rape complaint. He had taken his time to carve a flower into the small of her back. I flinched when I envisioned the pain she would have endured.

Then I flipped to the photos. The first one was black and white and looked nothing like him. The second one was even worse. How were these pictures of the same person? They had the same fingerprints, but he must be the master of disguise because I didn't recognize any of them.

I closed my eyes and took a deep breath, handing the folder back to Taylor. I shook my head to let him know that it wasn't any of them. He looked confused, glancing at the pictures himself. I saw the confusion on his face that matched mine. How could these pictures be of the same person?

There were case file numbers attached to each picture. Taylor walked out into the living area and used my laptop to pull the case file numbers. Each picture was a different guy. Someone had been able to get into the system and put them together with a fingerprint, which meant Mark and SWAT would come back empty-handed or with the wrong suspect.

I watched as events unfolded in slow motion. First, Taylor ran his hand through his hair and turned to talk to the officers. Then he picked up his phone and began shouting orders to shut down the systems at the *courthouse and our offices, as well as the police department.*

Everyone was going to go into a shutdown pattern while they brought in FBI specialists to find out how this happened.

I needed to get the sweat off me, and clear my head, so I grabbed my luggage and rolled it into the bathroom. I turned on the shower and waited for it to warm. I discarded my gun and purse; I had fallen asleep with them still on me. I dropped my clothes into a laundry bag and climbed in the shower.

I closed my eyes and envisioned Mark standing in the bathroom holding me, comforting me, even though it was because of him I was broken. I placed my hand on the wall as my sadness disappeared and anger stepped in.

I wouldn't be upset for the victims anymore. It was sad what had happened to them and their families, but if I was going to make it, and strap the murderer into the electric chair, I needed to be angry and get vengeance for what had happened to those people.

After finishing my shower, I dried and straightened my hair. I applied new make-up and painted my toenails. I then heard Kate through the bathroom door, so I put on my black mini skirt with my fishnets and black thigh high boots. I pulled on a white silk shirt that was baggy and hung off my shoulder. I had expected to have a girls night with Kate and looked like I was ready for the club. I made a mental note to get permission to return to my apartment for more appropriate clothes.

After spritzing on perfume, I was almost ready. My skirt was too short for my holster so I placed it on my waistband alongside the skirt. I laughed when I imagined Mark would tell me I looked like a kick-ass hooker. Taking a deep breath, I walked out the door.

Kate was in tears when I reached her. The last time I saw her, she thought I was dead.

"Hey Kate, you okay? You know it'll take a lot more than some killer with a hard-on for me to get me down."

I tried to smile at her, but she enveloped me in her arms and bawled on my shoulder. I hugged her back and whispered that everything would be all right.

"I am so sorry, Brook," Kate said in between her tears.

"Kate, you have no reason to be sorry. It's fine. I love you like a sister and I would be crying all over you if the roles were reversed."

Kate hugged me tighter and murmured something I couldn't make out. Then I looked over her shoulder to see two of the officers had red rings under their eyes. The others would not look at me. Taylor walked over and stood behind Kate and had his phone in hand. His expression told me something else happened while I was in the shower.

I pulled back from Kate and allowed her to hold my hand. I looked to my boss for whatever had everyone so upset. I placed my hand on my stomach when I thought it could be another victim. What if he had hurt that little boy I gave my phone to? I thought I was going to be sick.

Taylor's words sounded like gibberish through the roaring sound of my beating heart.

"What?" I asked, and tried very hard to calm my nerves so I could hear what had happened.

"Brooklyn..." My boss started to repeat himself but stopped to take a deep breath. It was never a good sign when my boss calls me by my first name. Whatever it was had him frazzled.

"Brooklyn, Mark has been shot. He has been rushed to New York-Presbyterian."

Everyone in the room seemed to shed a tear while I stood in silence. I was still inside the dream. That's what this was. My worst nightmare come to life.

"Is he alive?" I asked, wishing I could wake up and go back to the day I got my apartment. Everything was perfect and serene. Even Mark stopping by had been a perfect touch to the perfect day.

"We don't know. He was unconscious and they rushed him there. There will be no update until the Chaplain or his next of kin can get there."

Kate enveloped me into her arms and cried on me again. I stood tall and held her as if it wasn't real.

"His mother died. His dad and step-mom are in California." I took a deep breath. "He is an only child with no family here other than the department." My voice cracked as I tried to keep the tears at bay. "Can I qualify as his family?" I asked my boss as if he had any say in the matter.

"Let's just get you to the hospital and see."

CHAPTER
Nine

ANOTHER STORM HAD DESCENDED UPON New York this one was angrier than the last and seemed to want to stay over us. I stood under the emergency room overhang and watched the rain blow in. It had created a waterfall over the end of the awning.

I stuck my arm out and relished the cold water that poured down my arm. Before my mom died, she had once told me there was an old wives' tale about wishing on a star. The story says you should never wish on a star, that there is only one star everyone wishes on and it cannot keep up. She told me you make wishes in the water. Each drop can carry one wish and you have a better chance of your wish being heard.

I stepped into the waterfall and let the water cascade down my body as I made a wish. I wished I could stop this killer. I made a wish Mark would live. I made a wish my dad would walk the straight and narrow path so I would never have to visit him behind plexiglass again.

"Brooklyn?" I heard a voice call out my name as I stood in the water. I couldn't see who it was and I didn't care. The water was carrying my wishes away.

I started to say a prayer as well to make sure I covered every angle when I heard my name again. I closed my eyes and ran my hands down my hair, pushing it back from my face.

At that moment, lips crashed against mine. I could taste coffee and whipped cream. The same flavor I always tasted when Mark kissed me. I pushed him back and stepped out of the water to see him standing before me with a hello kitty band-aid on his forehead.

I looked him over and saw nothing else wrong with him. My emotions were mixed with disbelief and joy. The thought of him dying or leaving me was agonizing, and I needed him now.

I pulled him back out into the water and then dragged him across Madison Avenue into Marcus Garvey Park. I felt his hesitation when we passed the pools and walked through the trees. As we descended upon the baseball field, Mark had an idea of what it was I wanted.

He then led me to home plate and kissed me with the tenacity of a man deprived. With the trees and the weather we had all the privacy we wanted, but the thrill of being outside was still there. I dropped to my knees and pulled him down to his knees with me.

I was drenched by the rain and my thighs coated in my own heat. Mark laid down on the mound and I climbed on top of him. The cold rain did nothing for the fire burning in my skin. I reached between us and unbuckled his belt. I then unzipped his pants and pulled his cock out.

The thought of never having him inside me again flourished and I couldn't move fast enough. I lifted up and Mark's fingers found my clit through my underwear. I nearly crumbled as he rubbed the tight little bundle of nerves. I cried out as he ripped off my underwear. He stuck one finger inside me and I squeezed it, wanting more. I needed more.

"You're ready for me," Mark shouted as the thunder rumbled.

He pulled his finger out and I put his cock at my entrance. I slowly lowered myself down his length and found it difficult to get him all the way inside me. Mark tilted me back a little and he slid right in. I wiggled at the new position that had me filled to the brim with his hard member. Every time I breathed, it seemed his cock hit that bundle of nerves inside me.

"Mark, I am always ready for you. Don't you get it? I love you!" I began to slowly lift up, and then crashed back down. I repeated this again and again.

"Brooklyn!" Mark called out as I leaned back again and had him crashing into that rough patch behind my pussy. My walls vibrated with need as the intensity of the moment came to light. I grabbed my breasts and pinched my nipples through my wet shirt.

"Oh God," I screamed as lightning descended around us. I should have been mortified that we were out in public. I should have been scared that we might get struck by lightning, but I wasn't. I was never afraid of anything when Mark was with me.

Mark sat up and pulled my soaked blouse off and pulled my bra down. He took one nipple into his mouth without warning. My head fell back and I moaned into the sky as the rain danced on my face. He wrapped one arm around my waist and showed me the pace he wanted. It wasn't fast like the other times. It was slow.

"I love the way you taste," Mark declared, as he moved to my other breast.

I was going to orgasm just from those words. I continued to ride him on home plate as he kneaded and caressed my breasts. At times, he even bit down on my neck and pulled my hair.

"I love the way your skin turns rosy when you get turned on," Mark whispered in my ear before he bit down on my neck again.

I dug my fingers into his soaked clothes as I rode us higher and higher. My movements were growing sporadic as the need to climax increased.

"Mark," I called out and suddenly I was flipped onto my back. Mark was on top of me. He lifted my knees to hang over his forearms to get him deeper. Then he grabbed my ass and lifted my hips off the ground. I screamed and clawed at the ground as the new position had me squirming in ecstasy. I tried to pull off of him and he laughed.

"Where are you going, Brooklyn? Don't you want to finish what you started?"

I shuddered as moisture flooded me. The rain was only adding to the intimacy of the moment. I needed him and would do anything at this moment to have him. He owned me in every possible way.

"Yes, Mark, yes! Please...oh, God!"

My orgasm stole my breath, my mouth parted. My veins breathed fire as blood coursed through them quickly. My heart expanded its beats as my pussy walls tried to implant Mark inside me forever. I clamped down on him and came with the intensity of the sun.

I was sure my screams could be heard for blocks. I needed more, I needed less. I didn't know, but I didn't have to know because Mark was leading me through every crest that came. I shuddered and everything went dark.

I opened my eyes to find my body completely on the ground and a hardened male still waiting to finish.

"You all right?" Mark asked.

"Um, I think so. What happened?" I asked.

"You blacked out," Mark replied with a caveman smile on his face.

"Why?"

"My guess would be the massive orgasm I just gave you. You know that G-spot never gets enough attention. Maybe I should play with it again."

My cheeks flamed and my skin turned a shade of crimson, but it didn't last long as he began pushing in and out of me in a slow, methodical manner.

I rubbed my hands through his wet hair. I pulled his lips down to kiss me. At first it was a light peck and he lifted off me to look down.

He was gorgeous. The rain poured down around him and lightning shattered in the distance. The thunder rolled in sync with his pulsating cock. I was hopelessly in love with this man.

"Brooklyn, when you look at me like that I want to wrap you in bubble wrap to keep you from getting hurt," Mark whispered, before he sucked my earlobe into his mouth.

"God, Mark, you fit me perfectly," I murmured with no control over the words leaving my mouth.

He looked down at me again and I saw the look on his face. The look that said he would never be with me, that this was the last time I would ever have him inside me. My words had somehow stolen the spontaneity of the moment and turned it into a goodbye.

"Brook..." The veins in his neck and forehead protruded, telling me he was close.

"Mark, look at me when you come. Please, let me have that much," I whispered, as a tear streamed down my face. The rain helped to hide it, but Mark and I both knew it was there.

He kissed the tear falling on the side of my face and pumped into me faster. I felt the pulsing behind my clit once more. Mark altered his position slightly so he was hitting that spot over and over again.

I stared into his eyes as my body tightened down on him. My breasts swelled and felt heavy. I caressed his cheeks as the orgasm rammed into me. I kept my eyes locked on his as the waves of pleasure flowed through. It was a mixture of release and pain as the orgasm shattered my heart. I seemed to find myself here a lot lately, but I wouldn't trade this moment for anything.

I kissed Mark to drown out my cries and tightened down on him. The guttural moan he let out told me he was in the same ecstasy. He stared into my eyes as he pumped into me and came inside me. Then he bore down on me and kissed me as if he was starving for my lips.

I hadn't noticed the rain had stopped until he pulled out of me. I instantly felt empty again as he stood up and pulled me with him. I picked my soaked shirt up off the ground and pulled my skirt down while he fixed his pants.

"Brooklyn, we need to talk. It can't wait any longer. Let's go get dry clothes and have some coffee."

I nodded my understanding and let him take my hand and walk back to the hospital. Kate was waiting for us with Mark's Escalade.

"You guys are loud," Kate whispered as she smiled at me.

"We weren't doing anything," I replied with a smile on my face. I really wasn't in a laughing mood, but considering what could have happened to Mark, I would allow for Kate to lighten the mood.

"Geez, Mark, is your dick that big or did you stick her on a vibrating Harley and take her for a ride?" Kate winked at him and Mark's face didn't change. He had turned into the tin man and acted as though he didn't have a heart.

"Kate, we are going to drop you off at home, and go talk, if that's okay with you," I said.

"Actually, take me to your hotel. You have single cops waiting for you and I could use some company. Just bring wine when you come back to the room."

I nodded my acceptance, and Mark grabbed my hand, holding it while he drove.

"Mark, you can't scare us like that again. We thought you were dead," Kate said, as we headed for the hotel.

"So did I," Mark admitted.

"What happened?"

"It was a trap. We went to arrest this guy who was already dead. We saw him through the open door to his house. When we entered there were traps set up. I tripped on the door frame and fell back which is why I got a graze instead of a bullet in the brain." Mark squeezed my hand. God, I loved this man. Even in the face of that danger, he was there reassuring me. He was giving me comfort for his turmoil.

"What happens now?" Kate asked.

"We are now sharing the case with the FBI. They have the bomb squad, SWAT, and an EOD team in route to clear the house. They are having to evacuate part of the neighborhood before anyone else goes in. We don't want to risk losing more people or evidence that can lead us to his killer."

The ride was turning ominous. Everyone felt it, but no one said anything about it. I turned to Kate and gave her the biggest smile I could manage as my way of saying thank you to my friend. She stared at Mark holding my hand and back at me. I shook my head that there was nothing there, but she had to add her two cents.

"Mark, you know you two would make an adorable couple." Kate giggled.

"Is that so?" Mark responded sarcastically.

"Oh, yeah. I bet the sex would be hot and the babies would be adorable. You can't tell me you wouldn't want to see a bunch of little Brooks running around."

I turned to look at her with a pleading stare to stop, but she merely giggled harder.

"I think Brooklyn would have beautiful babies with anyone," Mark said. "She is gorgeous, and she would have no problem finding someone because she is like a fine wine. After one taste, any man would want her."

Kate took the bait and did what most friends do. Her attitude and mood did a one-eighty and she uttered the question that was rehashing what I was trying to put behind me.

"You have tasted her, so why don't you want her?" Kate asked, and I turned my head to look at her again. Her statement caused a tear to betray me and fall down my cheek. When Mark didn't answer her, she turned her giggles into anger.

"Let me get this straight. I can hear my best friend screaming your name from an orgasm nearly a block away, and you enjoyed that, but you wouldn't enjoy spending your life with her?" Kate asked with disdain dripping off her words.

"Kate, it's not like that," I whispered.

"Its fine, Brook," Mark answered, telling me not to say anything more. Kate huffed and before anyone could say another word she unbuckled her seat belt and climbed forward. I turned my head to look her in the eye, and she saw more than I wanted her to.

"Mark, pull over!" Kate demanded.

"Why?" Mark retorted.

"There is no way in hell you are being left alone with her again. You can call your little cop buddies, but I am taking her with me." Kate dismissed him and wrapped her arms around me.

I didn't want a scene, so I pleaded with her to sit back in her seat by whispering in her ear. Mark pulled into a parking garage and flashed his badge to get inside.

When the vehicle stopped, Kate climbed out and opened my door. She nearly ripped me from my seat as my seat-belt caught my arm. Mark got out and walked around the vehicle and leaned against it with his hands in his pockets.

"You don't deserve to breathe the same air as her. You men are all the same. As long as we are riding you, you never have to do any work. I can see she loves you and is doing all the work to try *not* to want you! So where are you, Mark? Where is your halfway point? When will you do any work?"

Kate growled and took out her cell phone to call a cab. Mark would not look at me, and I knew his intention was to say goodbye. I had thought that was what it was in the first place, but now I had confirmation.

I started to walk away, but turned around and walked back to Mark. Finally, he straightened up and opened his arms for me. No words had to be spoken as he held me. We both knew how the other felt. I started to pull away when he placed a kiss on my cheek and whispered in my ear. "I have always loved you."

I wept as Kate and I walked out of the parking garage. Would I be able to put it behind me to continue working with him? Would my boss let me step down if I couldn't? So many questions with no answers.

Kate hooked her arm around mine and laid her head on my shoulder as we walked up the incline to the parking garage. As we reached the top, a cab was waiting for us. Climbing in the back, we headed for the hotel.

Within minutes, we were followed by the police in marked cars to show that I still was not by myself even though I felt very much alone.

"Talk to me, Brookie," Kate whispered so the cab driver would not hear.

"What's to say? You heard and saw how he acted." I responded through sniffles from my tears.

"I thought you two were just friends. I leave you alone for a couple days and this turned into something else. Catch me up."

I proceeded to tell her the entire story before we got to the hotel. I didn't want his fellow officers to hear what happened or how he broke my heart. When I finished the story and wiped my tears, I looked to Kate to see what she thought.

Before she could get a word in the cab driver spoke up.

"Sounds like he is playing *games* with you." I looked through the glass and saw the glimmer of green eyes in the rear-view mirror.

"How do you keep following me?" I asked as I grabbed Kate's phone.

"Technology is a simple yet dirty thing," he replied, as I texted Mark to tell him our cab driver was the killer. "Just like that text you are trying to send won't send until you are out of the cab."

He smiled through the rear-view mirror at me and I felt sick. Then he held up the cell phone I had given to the little boy.

"It's fully charged. I thought you might like it back," he said.

"Am I going to be dropped off at my hotel or is this where you cut me and play with me before covering my body in blue flowers?"

It was at that moment that Kate realized who he was and pulled out her PDA to send an email. It was an older PDA and didn't bounce off the same towers as the new cell phones, but sadly he had been prepared for that. Kate pointed at the no signal sign on her PDA. She couldn't send a message, but we could record whatever was said in the cab.

"Brooklyn, I assure you I have no interest in killing you unless you decide not to play along," he answered.

"Why me?" I asked.

"You were the first girl I cared about. The first one to play a game with me."

I had no clue who this guy was and yet he knew me. Even his answers were somewhat cryptic because they seemed to carry a hidden meaning I just wasn't getting.

"Did you hurt that little boy?" I asked and then held my breath for the answer.

"No, he is fine. I am not an animal. Is that what you think of me? That I would hurt anything I came across that resembled you?" he asked, anger lacing his tone.

"I don't know you. I don't know what you are capable of, but I do know that every time I see a photo of a victim they look like me." I spoke softly, hoping not to piss him off while I was in the car.

"You do know me, Brooklyn, you just don't remember. You will remember everything soon."

As we pulled closer to the hotel I was tempted to get out and run with Kate, but he hadn't done anything to threaten me and yet again I felt threatened.

"Brooklyn, I don't ever want to hurt you. I would never hurt you the way Detective Stone has hurt you. I merely want to rid the world of the girls who try to be you."

I was stunned by his admission. I felt like this was a pet bringing me a dead animal and feeling proud for catching and killing it. He seemed to think on that same line as well.

"Similar DNA or a box of hair dye and colored contacts are not acceptable reasons to kill people," I said boldly. "Mark may have hurt me, but I went into the situation knowing he would. Those women, those victims, went into their day thinking they wouldn't be hurt, that they would be able to wake up and live another day. I will have days after Mark, but will you have days after I am done with you?"

I opened the door and stepped out of the cab. Kate stepped out with me, and he drove off without another word. The police car pulled up and I motioned for him to roll down his window. We told him the cab driver was the killer as we read off the cab number, and he took off into traffic following a river of cabs. There was no way to see which one it was now.

Kate used her PDA to send an email with the voice recording to Mark as we entered the hotel. I dropped her phone, my phone, and the PDA into a large envelope with the front desk and asked them to call the police to pick it up and leave us undisturbed.

We were going to dance the night away with a bottle of wine and a handful of cops.

CHAPTER
Ten

DAYS PASSED IN A BLUR. Kate only left me alone to go to work over the weekend. It was Monday morning and a decision had been made to have me step down from the case. I had refused to leave the hotel and Mark hadn't come around, so it was for the best.

I took a shower and dressed in a black jacket and black pencil skirt with a silk lilac halter top. I put on my knee high heeled boots and fixed my hair in long loose curls, then did my make-up.

I stepped out of the bathroom to find my dad and a half dozen cops keeping him away from me. I told them to let him in and my dad came forward, gracing me with a kiss on each cheek.

"Lyubov moya, you look tired. Is everything all right? You are not eating," he added, noticing the trays of untouched food. The truth was, I wasn't hungry. My emotions and the case had me drained.

"I am fine, Nikolas, just not sleeping well these days," I retorted.

"Please, how many times do I have to ask you to call me *dad?*" He pulled back a chair at the dining table where I joined him. I heard the sound of tearing paper, and Nikolas and I both looked under the table to see a copy of the note. The one Mark had dropped that night.

My dad picked it up and read it, then looked at me and read it again.

"Lyubov moya, who wrote this?"

"We don't know, but it doesn't matter to me because I am stepping down as the prosecutor on this case," I responded.

No one can seem to give me what I want. You won't walk away and continue to play the game you were not invited to. If you continue to play, I will make you part of the game.

There is one thing I want and she is like the sun over Brooklyn. Her hair is dark as night and eyes as blue as the ocean. Bring her to play and you may live to see another day.

My dad read the words out loud and I shivered with their meaning and intent. I watched as concern covered his face, and despite all that crap as I give him for being a criminal, I could honestly tell he cared for me.

"I used to say that to your mother." Nikolas sighed. "I want my men with you today." He spoke softly so the officers in the room would not hear him.

"I am covered, *Dad*," I said, attitude dripping off the word *dad*. "What was it you used to say to

Mom?" I asked, suddenly unsure what he was talking about, and wondering what the connection was.

"I used to tell her she was as beautiful as the sun over Brooklyn. It is partly how we got your name. Seems like it was yesterday when it was really a long time ago, Lyubov Moya."

Maybe he really missed my mom. He wasn't there when she got sick and died, so my sympathy for him ran thin when it came to her.

"I am uneasy about today," I said.

"Then let my men come, too. It is the least I can do to keep you safe."

"No, I have some things to say to Mark and don't want any extra ears around." I wiped at the tear that was betraying me as I brought up his name. My dad looked venomous at the mention of Mark combined with the look on my face.

"You tell Mark, a deal was a deal. After today, he doesn't see you again!" My dad gritted his teeth angrily. I got up and walked into the bedroom and wiggled my finger to tell him to come inside.

"Explain!" I demanded as I put my gun back in the holster and placed it on my waist. For added protection, I had a pocket sewn into my boot so no one could tell the pepper spray was hidden just inside.

"Lyubov moya, my love, why do you want to know these things that will make you think poorly of me?" Nikolas responded.

"Are *you* the reason?" I screamed at him without realizing my voice was that loud.

"Reason for what?" he asked, confusion on his face.

"Are you the reason he won't be with me? Are you the reason why I will never be good enough for him?"

I didn't want to admit it out loud, but it was the truth and I wanted to know if my dad had anything to do with it.

"Yes," Nikolas snapped. "He asked for a favor, and when I do a favor, I expect a favor. I did something for him and in exchange he had to stay away from you."

I felt the tears welling up inside me again. I turned my back on my dad and whispered words into the air that penetrated the thick silence. "I love him."

"Lyubov moya, you don't love him. You merely see him as your protector." Nikolas started to wrap his arms around me, but I spun around and spit in his face.

"I have loved him since we were kids. While you spent your days behind bars, dreaming of life on the outside, I was dreaming of a life with him."

Nikolas wiped the spit off his skin and took a step back. His face turned red when he shouted. "Ask him why I was in prison. I didn't do that for me!"

The cops took the opportunity to burst through the door due to all the yelling. I waved them away, letting them know everything was all right. As they backed out of the room, I turned to my dad. "If you are the reason I cannot have him in my life, then I do not want you in my life, either."

I watched as shock reverberated through my father over what I had said. He almost looked stricken. I felt sorry for him for a moment. I knew what it felt like to love someone so deeply and know it was not being returned. I know that was how my dad felt about me. I always knew he loved me, and I did a poor job of showing him I loved him because of the life he chose, but he was still my father.

I would always love him even if he wasn't in my life. Fifteen years in prison proved that. I grabbed my purse and headed out of the room. I was escorted by all but a few officers who stayed to keep my room safe while I was gone.

I was led outside and into a waiting Escalade. I was shocked to find Mark and Taylor up front in the vehicle when I got inside.

"You ready, Ms. Montgomery?" Taylor asked.

When Taylor acted as my boss he was a stubborn, arrogant man, but when I caught him outside of work, he was a wonderful, understanding person. It didn't take much after hearing the recording on the PDA to get him to allow me to step aside. Lately, he was more of a friend and confidant than a boss.

"Ready as I will ever be," I answered.

We were waiting for the rest of the convoy to be loaded when my dad came out of the hotel. He looked at the tinted windows and blew a kiss before walking down to the valet.

That was that. My dad blowing a kiss was the equivalent of a goodbye. I would miss his Russian pet names for me, but I wouldn't miss being investigated because of him.

"You okay?" Mark asked, when he saw the expression on my face.

"Yeah, it's just time to make a few changes in my life."

I wasn't going to discuss it with my boss in the car because I didn't know what kind of favor my dad did for Mark.

We rolled down to the courthouse and I was carted inside by an army of police and FBI. All of them looking for the same man who, in my experience, did well blending in with his surroundings. He could be one of them, for all I knew.

After a meeting with the commissioner, the mayor, and the deputy director of the FBI, I had to brief the other Assistant District Attorneys on the case and where we were. It seemed like I had been at this for days when it had only been a few hours.

Everywhere I went, my body was on alert and I never went anywhere alone. I even had four officers stand outside the bathroom while I peed. This was just another reason to step down.

The five o'clock hour was coming up fast, and at five-thirty all the local news networks would be live while I told the city of New York that it was somehow my fault this psycho was killing their loved ones. There had not been any more victims, but that didn't mean he was done.

I finished briefing the paralegals and going over details when I pulled the torn paper from my briefcase and read it aloud to the staff.

Mark was standing guard at the door and we stared at each other as I read it. Remembering that night was beautiful yet painful. I had come to find that a little pain was worth it if it brought pleasure, and Mark definitely delivered. But the pain I felt at losing him now overrode that pleasure.

That was the thing about life. No one ever asks you what you want. You merely have to pave the path and hope no sinkholes open up to deter you from where you are headed.

I stood inside the glass doors of the courthouse and stared at the forming crowd on the stairs. My nerves were starting to fire up and the butterflies swarmed in my stomach. My palms grew sweaty and my mouth went dry. I tried to clear my throat, but sudden dehydration made it hard to function.

I felt my palm grow warm like fire and looked down to see that Mark was holding my hand. He was always there when I needed comfort, even when he was the reason I was upset.

"Mark, you should have told me," I whispered.

He took the opportunity to study my face, and he realized I knew something. He pulled my hand and dragged me inside one of the briefing rooms where lawyers and clients went to try to discuss cases or option plea deals.

Once the door was shut, he walked up to me and pushed me against the wall. He pinned my arms above my head and spread my legs with his. I felt the throb behind my clit as his lips fell over mine and I opened to him. I had missed him and missed this. I didn't realize how much until I tasted the coffee and whipped cream. I would never be able to stomach a coffee shop without him in my life. I moaned as his tongue penetrated my mouth and caressed my tongue.

He released my hands to run his hands up and down my body. I grabbed his brown silky hair and stood up on my tip-toes to get more. Mark wrapped his arms around me and held me tight. It was all so surreal I thought I was dreaming again. Only instead of a nightmare it would be a dream to beat all dreams.

Mark pulled back and laid his forehead on mine as he caught his breath. A single tear rolled down my cheek when I saw the redness in his eyes. I felt empty and needed him to fill me back up. I wasn't whole unless I was with him.

"Brooklyn, I love you. I think the sun rises and sets with you. There is never going to be another like you. I will never be half the man I am when I am with you. I would do anything that was possible to ensure you are happy. I crave every second I can steal with you, but it is an ill-gotten victory because I know that moments like this one will become a distant memory.

I made a promise that I cannot break or I would lose you anyway."

I didn't get a chance to say anything before he walked out the door. My nerves were unraveled now, yet I felt a smidgen of confidence peeking through. Mark had a way of making me feel as if I was Wonder Woman. Now it was time to put that confidence to work.

I pulled out a mirror from my purse and fixed my lipstick. Then I walked out and saw they were all waiting for me. The mayor was making her speech, and I was up next. I stared at the glass, making the people turn blurry while I tried to remember what it was the state wanted me to say.

I heard my name and opened the door to make my descent down the stairs. As I neared the microphone, I saw Mark watching me and I locked eyes with him.

"My name is Brooklyn Montgomery. I am the current Assistant District Attorney assigned to oversee the progress and prosecution of the Cut-Me-Not case."

Now came the hard part. I took a deep breath and looked back up to see bright green eyes smiling at me. He was here. He stood a foot away from Mark and my dad was on the other side. All I needed was Kate and my dream would come full circle around me. I focused in on the killer so he would know I was speaking to him.

"It was brought to my attention that I was assigned to this case at the request of the perpetrator. This is not how the State of New York works. We as a nation do not negotiate with terrorists, so it would stand to reason that the State of New York would not bypass the standard in which things are done because a local terrorist has demanded that I take over the case."

I definitely had his attention now. His smile faltered and he looked murderous. He pushed up so that I could see the knife that hung on his belt. He was very good at blending in because no one noticed him.

"As of today, I have briefed both the NYPD and the FBI and every ADA who will be taking over this case. To ensure that it will be done correctly, there will be three prosecutors looking over this case instead of one and they will remain nameless for their own safety."

I knew my time was nearing an end, but I wasn't quite finished while I had everyone's attention.

"I know most of you will insist on calling me the 'Mafia Lord's Daughter' or something to that effect. I want you all to know when you print the article you should print the truth. You can even quote me on this. Everyone who works in this job does it for the pleasure that comes with the pain. It is devastating to hear the stories, and relate to the victims' families, but we do it every day because the cause is greater than our own needs. It is painful to come to work each day knowing that we only have a job because of the bad out there in the world. I don't think I could function if this job were only pain. The pleasure we get is when we see victims get justice. While it may not help the victim or their family, we get pleasure knowing one more criminal is off the streets, and this helps us sleep a smidgen easier at night."

Time to bring the conversation to a close. Green Eyes had his knife in his hand, but a perplexed look on his face. Mark stared at me intently as if absorbing everything I was saying into a different context just for him. My dad seemed to understand what I was trying to say, and reporters everywhere were scribbling down little notes and holding up recorders.

"In conclusion, I hope one day I can return to the District Attorney's office. I hope I can serve my city and bring justice to those who need it. But at this time there is no pleasure in my job. Since the perpetrator has singled me out and left the blood on my hands it is agony to continue in the office. I pray for the families of the victims and pray there are no more. This is not a game, this is real life, and we all need some good with the bad."

My boss walked up and waved at the reporters as he placed his hand on the small of my back.

"He's here," I murmured, and Taylor moved me over and spoke into the microphones.

"Any questions?" he asked.

The reporters began shouting loudly and I waited until Taylor released me before I took the opportunity to head back up the stairs. With the reporters chaotically asking rapid questions, no one noticed the green-eyed man who came forward past Taylor.

I looked to Mark, who was trailing up the stairs. It seemed he knew what was happening, yet he wasn't rushing to help me. The mayor looked over and saw what was happening, too, but she made no move to help me, either. It seemed I was on my own. I used my voice and screamed loud enough to make the reporters all look in my direction.

I took a few steps to the side and told the reporters the man was a potential suspect and they had free reign to ask anything they wanted. As the reporters flooded him with questions, putting lots of people between his knife and my flesh, I hurried outside toward Mark's Escalade. Something else was making me uneasy.

At the last moment, I decided I would take the subway. I hadn't had any real freedom in weeks so thirty minutes in the subway would be a welcome change.

I got down the block and crossed the street when a black Escalade pulled up beside me.

"Get in, Brooklyn," Mark called out as the setting sun pierced my eyes with its brightness.

"I am fine, Mark, go home," I answered, still feeling uneasy.

"Either you get in or I will put you in here."

I kept walking, which was apparently not the right thing to do. Within a few seconds I was being lifted over Mark's shoulder and carried to the passenger seat of the Escalade.

He dumped me in my seat and buckled the belt. I tried to get out when I heard my dad from the back seat.

"Lyubov Moya, don't go," he said, stopping me from pulling the handle and running away.

I crossed my arms and leaned back in the seat. I watched out the window as we headed to my hotel room. I never wanted to repeat this day, or experience anything like it again.

"Brooklyn, I am going to clear your room for an hour. We all need to talk." Mark spoke softly.

I merely rolled my eyes and went back to daydreaming. I watched the sky as it darkened, matching my mood. I loved the nighttime air in New York, and the way it imposed a different atmosphere once the sun set. Everything that happened after night fell contrasted with everything that happened when the sun shined its brightest on my favorite city.

The only thing I hated about my city was the missing stars. I didn't want them to make a wish on, but I missed lying on the grass and staring at them like I did when my mom took me to my grandmother's farm in northern Kentucky. There were so many stars at night on the farm that I would drift off to sleep counting them.

"Instead of you two waiting, just tell me so I can go to my room to get away from you both," I said as we neared the hotel. Mark let out a sigh and looked into the rear-view mirror at my dad.

"Brooklyn, you know my mother was murdered. The District Attorney decided not to press charges because he didn't want to ruin his conviction rate. I went to your dad for help." Mark's lips moved, and I heard the words that came out, but was unaware of what it had to do with me. Then the light bulb went off and I knew.

"I grew up without my dad for ten years because you needed justice for your mother?" I stated it like a question, hoping they knew it was rhetorical. I was angry, but it also explained a lot.

Growing up, I had known what kind of stuff my dad was involved in, but he had lackeys to get their hands dirty so he didn't have to. I never understood why he participated in the torture of that man. I never could find the connection between my dad and him, and now I knew.

"So, let me get this straight, your mom gets killed by some psycho and you go to my dad to ask him to have the man tortured and killed. Then my dad tells you the only way he would do it is if you stayed away from his only daughter?"

I waited and they both murmured that I was kind of correct. My fury exploded.

"Are we on *Days of our* damn *Lives* or some other soap opera? Because that is the *only* way I see that information being helpful in this scenario. Do you have anything else to tell me? No, scratch that. I don't want to know any more. Mark, you broke my heart so your mom could rest in peace, and while I understand it, you should have let the justice system do its job or grown a set to do it yourself. Nikolas, you committed a torturous act on someone because you saw where Mark and I were headed as we aged, didn't you?"

I sat back in my seat and willed tears of anger not to fall. I had done enough crying; I was like a weeping baby because of the two of them.

"I went to your dad because I did do it. I'm the one who tortured him," Mark admitted. "Your dad just led the evidence in a different direction, but we made a mistake and they pinned it on him."

The words hit me hard.

"Brook, I love you. I only did what was best for you," Nikolas said.

"Except I fell in love with Mark and gave him my heart. Now, thanks to the both of you, I will be picking up the pieces of that shattered heart for years to come. You can both go to hell, because we are done!"

CHAPTER
Eleven

T HE NEXT DAY, I CHECKED out of the hotel and ditched my phone. I cleaned out my bank account and gave the officers the slip. I was grateful to my father that I knew how to get away unscathed.

I took a cab and went to my apartment. I was surely going to miss it. I laid out my suitcases and packed everything that was important, then gathered pictures of my mom and me when we built sand castles on the beach. I missed her every day, but everyone told me to be grateful she wasn't in pain anymore.

I was glad her pain was gone, but mine had begun the day she got sick. I took a bottle of wine from the refrigerator and opened it. It wasn't long before she got sick that I had welcomed Mark with open arms. His family had moved into the neighborhood and I immediately took to the brown haired little boy who would come over to play.

When my mother died and my dad went to prison, Mark's dad took me in and became a father figure while I waited for my aunt to come and raise me. On weekend visits to see my dad in prison, I would be so emotionally strung out that I would sneak out at night and climb into bed with Mark. Even at the age of seven he would hold me and let me cry on his shoulder, telling me everything would be okay.

I chugged the first glass of wine and went to my closet to pull down a box of miscellaneous things from the past. I opened it and found photo albums of

Mark and me. I found my mother's veil. I poured everything out and chugged another glass of wine.

I played with the Rubix cube I made with Mark. We tore off all the stickers and used glow in the dark paint to sign our names on the cube. I reached over and turned out the lights to see it still said 'Mark & Brooklyn FFL.'

It was in our adolescent years when we wrote that we were friends for life on everything. Funny how when I look back on it now, I have no regrets except for how it ended.

I no longer had my dream job at the District Attorney's office. I would never be able to afford this apartment unless I found a great job, maybe in corporate law, so criminals wouldn't single me out again.

I felt like I had just unpacked my life and it was time to go again. I would never move on with my life if I stayed, even if I found a great job. Mark would still have my heart and I couldn't imagine living my life that way.

I heard my doorbell and chugged down another glass of wine before opening it. I opened the door to see Mark standing there. I didn't even bother to turn on the light or welcome him in. I merely closed the door and went to pour myself another drink.

"Brooklyn, please," Mark called out.

"It's not locked you know," I shouted back. My brain told me to make him leave, but my heart wanted to see him again. I was pouring another glass of wine when he walked inside and closed my door.

"You should always keep your door locked. It's not safe," Mark stated.

"What exactly do I have left to protect?" I responded, hoping the meaning would be understood without further explanation.

Mark walked toward the kitchen where I was drinking my wine as fast as I could pour it. He stepped up behind me and pinned me to the island.

I gulped down the rest of my wine as he moved my hair to the side and flung it over my shoulder. I poured another glass as I felt his lips on my neck and his hands caressing my breasts. I knew I should stop him. I knew I would only get hurt, but after I felt his hardening length behind me all reasoning went out the window.

I gulped down the wine in my cup and poured another with shaking hands, moaning as he pulled my shirt out of my jeans. I went to pour more, but Mark reached around and took the cup from my hand and set it aside.

"Do you really want to be drunk right now?" he whispered as he unbuttoned my pants.

I felt his hand graze down my smooth mound and find my entrance with his fingers. The first soft rub of my clit and I leaned over the island. I wanted to grind into his hand, but I wanted to resist as well.

My body and my hormones were at war with my heart and my restraint. I gasped as he moved lower and glided one finger inside me. He immediately went for the rough patch. I felt his other hand grab my pants and lower them ever so slowly while I panted on the island.

"Tell me you want me, Brook," Mark whispered as he kissed me between my neck and shoulder. I couldn't say a word; I merely moaned.

"Tell me we are not over yet," Mark added a second finger and I grabbed the edge of the island with a tightened grip.

"I love you, Brooklyn. You cannot run away from me," Mark whispered as he added a third finger.

I tried to claw the island and run away, but my body betrayed me and pushed back into him. When he pulled his hand out to spin me around, I took the opportunity to catch my breath.

He lifted me onto the island after removing all of my clothing, except my shirt and my panties. I watched as he licked his fingers before he pulled my shirt up over my head. I was mesmerized by him.

"God, Brooklyn your skin has lit up for me. It's beautiful," he whispered as he pulled my hair back and bit down on my neck. He kept my hair in place with my head aimed at the ceiling while he moved his lips down my chest.

"Mark—" My words were cut off when he pulled my tightened pink nipple into his warm mouth. The velvet feel of his tongue had me squirming on the island. He released my hair long enough that I tried to talk.

"Mark, I—" My sentence was cut short as he tugged my hair lightly and bit down on my nipple. I screamed out with shocked pleasure. My clit was pulsating, and I couldn't breathe. My brain went cloudy and I knew once I succumbed to the fog of ecstasy I would be at a loss for words.

As Mark moved his lips down my abdomen, I knew where he was headed and this was the only opportunity I had to tell him.

"Mark, I'm leaving!" Everything stopped at that moment. He acted as though I'd burned him. He stopped everything he was doing and stepped back against the counters.

"What?" he asked with shock in his voice.

"I leave on the first thing, flying out in the morning," I whispered as I crossed my legs when the pulsating didn't seem to calm down.

"Where are you going?" Mark asked with concern.

"Anywhere but here."

"When are you coming back?" he asked, and his eyes glistened in the light. I didn't have to answer because he already knew.

"Because of me?" Mark asked, seeming to catch his breath.

"What did you expect, Mark? Did you expect me to go on with life here without you in it? Did you expect me to sit at home and pray for you to drop by and give me some dick? You and my dad decided my fate years ago when you murdered someone. I need to move on and I need to do it away from those I have to cut out of my life."

My words came out crass, but my emotions were wrapped inside my words. I think I would always love him, but I couldn't be with someone who didn't want me the way I wanted him. Life is a commitment to do better, to be better. I couldn't do that without love and support from a man who stays by my side, not one who lurks in the shadows, looking for pussy during the night.

"Don't go," Mark whispered, but he refused to look at me.

"I will give you tonight, but in the morning I am gone!" The alcohol finally started to warm my belly.

I climbed off the island to be enveloped in those strong arms. I didn't look into his gorgeous blue eyes because if I did I might change my mind. I surrounded my senses with him and memorized every muscle and scent. I wanted to keep this night in my memory for when I got lonely.

I took his hand and led him into my bedroom. Mark pulled his shirt up over his head. He remained standing by the edge of the mattress, and I climbed onto the bed and over to him on my knees. I came face to face with his cobalt eyes and my heart fluttered. I planted a kiss on his neck and then on his shoulder. Mark let me have my fill of him.

I dropped my head and licked a circle around his nipple. I reached my finger up to pinch it lightly as I caressed and nibbled over each rock hard ab that showed me the way. By the time I got to his pants, I was bent over on all fours.

Mark placed a hand on my back so I dropped my chest lower and he walked around the bed. I watched between my legs as he dropped his pants and climbed up on the bed. I thought he was going to put his cock inside me, but instead I felt his tongue enter me. I gripped the bed sheets as his fingers found my clit.

I was in euphoria as his tongue rode me. I didn't even hear the door close as he moved farther up and ran a circle around my anus. It was the forbidden valley. I was an anal virgin and had every intention of staying that way until I felt his finger find entry into me, and coat juices up to my butt.

I swore I saw someone walking toward the bedroom, but my voice faltered to make any noise. I felt his cock at my entrance and he pushed in slowly as his finger pushed past the ring of muscles around my anus.

My lungs found their voice and screamed out in need. I wiggled and maneuvered. I wasn't sure if it was to get him out of me or to get more in. I lifted my head in my fog of desire to see my boss standing across from us with a file and a hard-on. I felt the moisture stream down my thighs as soon as I knew we were being watched.

"Beg him to stay," Mark whispered in my ear as he pulled my hair back. I flushed crimson as I was scandalized. The thrill was there under the utter embarrassment. I was leaving in the morning and wanted this to be different so the embarrassment had no place here in the room.

"Taylor, please," I screamed out as Mark nearly pulled all the way out of me.

"She likes an audience. She likes her sex on display."

Taylor walked in and took a seat in my computer chair after rolling it in front of me. His eyes glowed with a mischievous glare, but his stance said he was nervous like he had never seen a porn in his life. I watched as he rubbed his hand over his cock as Mark drove back into me.

"Mark—" I groaned as two fingers entered my anus and his other hand found my clit. My body was in a rocket shooting for the moon. Taylor leaned forward and pulled my face to kiss me. He tasted of caramel, a flavor that matched his skin.

Mark was pushing into me brutally as if marking his territory again. I loved it. I used one hand to pull at Taylor's pants. As I realized what this was turning into, I soaked the sheets with the moisture that flowed. Mark didn't like it at all. He lifted me so my back was to his chest and he pushed in and out of me with harsh vigor. He removed his finger from my anus and used both hands to knead my breasts.

Taylor held his long cock in his hand and began to stroke it while watching me. I felt like an enigma. I felt beautiful and confident that two men would be hard for me. I turned my head and kissed Mark with a moan flowing from my lips.

"Please," I begged, not knowing what I wanted. Not knowing what I needed. Mark growled but laid me on my side on the edge of the bed. I reached down between my legs, taking the moisture that was flowing like a river and transferring it to Taylor's lips. He sucked my finger in and groaned with my flavor. I did it again but instead of his lips I covered his cock with my hand and began to stroke him with my juices.

Mark growled in my ear, "You're mine," and I turned my head back and whimpered.

"Tonight I belong to you both." The words were out of my mouth before I could call them back. It was at that moment I realized this was never about being watched. This was about making him jealous. To make Mark see what he would be missing.

I bent forward, leaving my hips still, and pulling for Taylor. He stood and my mouth lunged for his cock. I pulled him in deep, to the back of my throat. Mark gritted his teeth and reached around to stroke my clit. I screamed around Taylor's cock as Marks movements grew rougher.

He pulled me off Taylor and laid me on my back with my head hanging off the bed.

"Tell me you want me," Mark growled.

He was not okay with any of this, but I was in a world all my own and said nothing. I reached and pulled Taylor to my mouth as my head hung off the bed. I pushed his hardened buttocks into me so his cock dove into my mouth.

I heard the grunt and felt the come pour into me from Mark, but he never slowed or faltered in his movements. I reached down and cupped Taylor's balls as his cock moved in and out of my mouth.

Taylor reached forward slowly and grabbed my breasts.

Mark lifted my hips to grind into that spot behind my apex. I moaned around Taylor's cock in my mouth. Mark pulled me off Taylor again and flipped me so he was on his back and I was mounted on top of him. It was my turn to do the work, but I wanted more.

"Taylor, please." I begged for him to come and join.

Taylor walked around the bed. He climbed on the edge and grabbed my breasts from behind me and kneaded them. He moved to the side and brought his head down and sucked one nipple into his mouth. I took the opportunity and sank my fingers into his soft black hair.

In this position, Mark had to see it all. He had to see that someone else wanted me. That I didn't have to wait for him. I wanted him to see I didn't need him, that it had been a choice to have him.

Taylor's fingers found my clit and I began to ride Mark slowly. I went with the rhythm that Taylor had on my clit. Mark pulled me down so Taylor couldn't get to my clit any longer. Taylor moved to the back of us and I thought he was gone until I felt his tongue pierce my anus.

"Oh, God," I screamed in unexpected pleasure. My orgasm was going to kill me. It was just building up higher than ever before.

"Mine," Mark called out.

"She wants it," Taylor replied.

Mark began driving into me and holding me in place above him while Taylor moved in sync with his tongue in my backside. I was off floating on cloud nine. Mark kissed me and I devoured his coffee flavor. I had never felt like this before. Mark slowed as I felt something big at my anus. I felt it push into me and gritted my teeth at the burn.

"Breath out and push back into me," Taylor said. I could feel them both inside me. I was stuffed full. I wanted to scream for him to pull out, but my body wouldn't let me. The look on Mark's face was murderous as I leaned down to kiss his neck.

"Sometimes the pain is worth the pleasure," I whispered in his ear.

I could see the hurt behind the anger in his eyes. I knew he loved me, and maybe this was pushing him too far, but I was enthralled with every moment of it.

It took the guys a few trial and error movements to get into a rhythm that would fit their needs and mine. One moved in as the other moved out. This is what heaven felt like.

My ears roared with the sound of my heart. My brain disappeared behind the fog of euphoria. My body stretched to accompany what was happening with an electricity that reached out to every nerve ending. The pain subsided and was replaced with agonizing pleasure. I clamped down on both of them as I tried to fend off the orgasm. It was too large, it would flatten me.

Mark reached down and lifted me just enough to find my clit. He rubbed that little bundle of nerves until I couldn't take it anymore.

"Mark..." I screamed as the orgasm exploded through me.

It was so intense I went out of body and looked down on what was happening. I could see everything so clearly. I could see the love Mark had for me, but I also saw the infatuation Taylor felt for me. I must have been blind to have missed that. I could see the poetry in what the three of us were doing. It was like moving art and it was intimate and beautiful.

When my body crashed back down to earth, my skin was on fire, my body ached with waves of need, my heart fluttered with renewed hope, and everything became overly sensitive. I gasped for the breath that was stolen from me.

When I tried to climb out of the elation in my head, I realized they were both achieving their release and I slumped forward onto Mark's chest as darkness fell upon me.

CHAPTER
Twelve

I COULD SEE THE NIGHT sky through the window from my bed. I felt boneless, satiated, and sore. I looked around to discover no one was around, yet I was naked and tucked into bed. I stretched to feel my muscles protest after the workout I had today. I climbed out of bed and went to the shower.

I took my time, making sure every bit of me was clean. What happened earlier was as intoxicating as it was demeaning. After scrubbing everything down twice, I climbed out of the shower and began to get ready for my flight.

I straightened my hair and put on my make-up. I pulled out a blue jean skirt and a white halter top to match my white cowboy boots. I was headed to Kentucky so I thought maybe I should look more southern than northern.

I packed another suitcase that I would use as a carry-on and then exited my bedroom. I saw both Taylor and Mark sitting at the island in the kitchen and my cheeks warmed. I was sure my skin flushed a deep maroon.

I rolled my bags to the door and walked around to talk to them. I noticed the clock on the wall said it was midnight. I still had five hours before my flight, but to keep my clothes on and legs shut, I needed to make this quick and get away from them.

They both stood as I came around the corner. They had been drinking coffee and discussing whatever was in the envelope on the counter-top.

"Don't go," Mark pleaded. I walked over to him and wrapped my arms around him. I let the tears flow as I said goodbye to the best friend I ever had. I turned to Taylor and enveloped him in my arms.

"We could have had so much fun together," I whispered in his ear and gave him a kiss on the cheek and a wink that told him how full of it I was.

"Ms. Montgomery, I would never steal you away. You belong to another, but let me say that tonight you gave me a lot more than I bargained for when I walked through your door," Taylor said softly as he kissed my knuckles.

"That is where you are wrong, Taylor. I only belong to myself," I told him, keeping the cracking in my voice to a minimum.

"I need to go, so will you guys lock up?" I asked as I pulled away from them and wiped the tears from my face.

"Let me drive you," Mark said.

"Saying goodbye to you twice is pure torture," I replied.

"Sometimes the pain is worth the pleasure," Mark responded, using my words.

"I will come, too...if it makes it easier, Brooklyn," Taylor offered.

I holstered my weapon and placed it on my hip. The good thing about having friends everywhere was that the Air Marshal was going to hold my gun during the flight so I would never be without it on the ground. Since there was an open threat against me from the Cut-Me-Not killer, the marshal agreed to assist me.

"Come on then, both of you." I let them grab my bags as we exited my apartment. I locked the door and we all gathered into the elevator. The tension was thick in the small confined space.

"You both smell like pussy," I spoke loudly, with a giggle, and the tension seemed to lighten up.

Taylor stuck a finger in his mouth and made a fake groan.

"I taste like one, too. Yum."

Now we were all laughing about it. The awkwardness was gone and the tension dissolved by laughter.

I really didn't think it was all that funny, but whatever made this easier for them was a good thing. They still had to work together after I left.

We piled into the Escalade. I had refused the police escort to the airport. Mark's actions spoke to how uneasy he was about my choice.

He kept looking everywhere and even buckled me into place. He and Taylor climbed into the SUV and we headed toward the airport. Mark was overly cautious and observant as he drove down the interstate.

Everyone and everything around him was suspect. Paranoia clung to him like smoke to a fire.

Every second moved slowly, as if we were walking instead of going eighty miles per hour.

I could time his actions. Every three seconds he would check his side mirrors. Every five seconds he would check the rear-view. Every ten seconds he would glance over his shoulder, seeking out that blind spot most vehicles have. Finally, every thirty seconds, he would glance over at me, all the while watching the road in front of him.

I hated that he felt like he had to be on guard with me like this, but the press release had come with several threats from those who claimed to be the killer. There were a few attention seeking people who had written threats that had nothing to do with me or the case, but Mark took each one of them seriously.

"You know I have a gun," I said with a smile that reached my eyes.

"I know you have a gun. I have one, too." Mark never took his eyes off his rotation.

"I bet mine is prettier than yours," I said with a giggle.

"Maybe, but mine is bigger than yours," Mark replied, and shot me a crooked smile.

"Mine tastes better," I retorted.

"Are we still talking about your gun?" Mark asked, and Taylor joined in the laughter.

"Taylor, I am going to miss your stubborn ass," I said with a smile.

"Brooklyn, I will merely miss your ass." We all chuckled about the implied meaning behind the sentence.

"Mark, I am going to miss giving you blue balls," I stated, with a wink in his direction.

"When did you give me blue balls?" Mark asked with genuine curiosity.

"I think it started in 1995 and lasted up until a few weeks ago," I stated. Mark and Taylor laughed, and soon Mark's paranoid techniques were behind us.

It was a smooth, carefree ride from there. I saw where they were doing construction on the interstate and we were having to detour through Brooklyn.

"Can we stop at the bridge for just a few minutes?" I asked, and Mark nodded his head.

"What is the story with you and the bridge?" Taylor asked.

"When I was little I remember my dad telling my mom that her smile was brighter than the sun setting on Brooklyn. I didn't even remember it until my dad brought it up. Then I remembered right before my dad went to prison he brought me out to the bridge and told me that the bridge was one of the Seven Wonders of the World. As I aged, I realized he was lying. I confronted him about it one Saturday during visitor's hours. He said the bridge was, in fact, one of the seven wonders of the industrial world. He said he named me after the bridge for all the beauty she maintained, as well as her strength. She killed many people on her way to perfection and he said that symbolized me. How I never let anyone stand in my way. As a tradition, every time I have left the city,

I have gone out and made a wish on the water for safe travels."

Mark took my hand in his. We rolled out toward the bridge and parked about a block away. Mark pulled an extra gun out of his glove box, and Taylor put it in his jeans and covered it with his shirt.

I took both of them by the hand and led them to the bridge. She was a glorious sight at night. Her lights showed her height and beauty. There was another storm off in the distance and the lightning dancing across the sky made her nearly picture perfect. I let them both go and walked to the middle of the bridge. I stood near the rail and inhaled the moist air.

I was going to miss home, but it was better for everyone if I left. I hadn't told anyone exactly where I was going so no one could be put in harm's way. I didn't plan to stay in Kentucky long, anyway. I was going to make sure I made a trip out to California to see Mark's father and step-mom. I would never go back for holidays, but I could make impromptu visits to see how they were.

Mark was on his cell phone and his face had fallen. My guess was there had been another victim. I closed my eyes and breathed in the air. The wind lifted my hair and I felt a hand on the small of my back.

"Brooklyn, you look so beautiful and carefree here and now," Taylor said, and I smiled. "Can I kiss you?" he asked sweetly.

"You know my heart belongs to Mark," I whispered as he grew closer.

"I wasn't asking for your heart," Taylor replied.

I looked over at Mark, who was oblivious to anything happening around him. I felt like this kiss would be betraying him, yet he openly told me he couldn't be with me.

Taylor leaned in and pressed his lips to mine. He pulled my body to him, his hands cupping my face.

He tasted of caramel, but I had a sudden urge for coffee and whipped cream. I pulled away and looked into his green eyes.

"Are you really going to run out on him?" Taylor asked, holding my hips in his hands.

"What's done is done. He can't change the past and I refuse to give up my future for a few hours of his cock per week. I deserve more than that."

I pulled away and leaned back against the rail. The winds blew my hair in scattered directions, and I could hear the horn of a tugboat nearing.

"What if I gave him immunity?" Taylor whispered.

"What?" I turned back to hear him out.

"I know, Brooklyn. He is one of the best we have on the force. Someone like him gets looked into from time to time. I know what happened." Taylor spoke quietly, and chills flew down my spine. "I know he was seven when his mom died. I know he was fourteen when he found out who killed his mom. I know it was Mark who tortured the man to death. I know your dad didn't do it but stepped up so a fourteen-year-old wouldn't have to go to prison over a passionate crime."

I looked over at Mark, who was on the phone shouting orders to the men he commanded. I could hear it in his voice that there was another victim. I hadn't listened when Mark had said he was the one who killed him. I merely wanted to keep blaming my dad and hold onto that anger. Standing here and staring at Mark, I could see it in him. I could see him killing for someone he loved.

"Would you stay if I granted him immunity?" Taylor asked again.

"Why would you do that?" Nothing is just a random act of kindness anymore.

"I have a few things I want from you. After today, there are a few more things we can add to the list, but the question is...how much do you love him?"

I wondered if I loved Mark enough to sell my body in exchange for his freedom. I loved him more than anything else, but giving up my body to Taylor would break him and he didn't deserve that.

"Tell me your price," I whispered, just so I had something to think about.

"First, you would stay here in New York. You would work alongside me in the District Attorney's office. You are a good lawyer, so never let it be said you didn't earn your position. Second, I want you to allow the FBI to use you as bait for the Cut-Me-Not killer. This is a high profile case, and we need to show the city of New York that we can handle this internally. I will even let you put the needle in the bastard's arm if you want."

So far, none of this sounded bad except for the bait part. Usually, the bait gets eaten before it can lure anything out of hiding. I saw the look on his face that I had seen on many men before. He was about to throw in the parts I didn't think I could survive.

"I will clear your dad's record and give immunity to Mark. I can even talk to the commissioner about a promotion because Mark is one of the best we have. If you agree to those two things, and a few others things, I can make this happen."

I swallowed and looked at Mark. He had his hand on his hip and was watching me intently. Did he know what we were talking about, or was his phone call that bad? I had to make a decision. My dad couldn't hold him to whatever deal they made if Taylor got them both cleared of any wrongdoing.

"What else would I have to do?" I asked, dreading the answer. It's one thing when I give my body up willingly; it's another matter when it is used as a negotiation piece. The lawyer in me knew what he was doing was immoral and wrong, but he had powers I didn't have.

"You make yourself available to me in any way at any time I deem necessary. I will own you. I may never call on you for anything, or I may call you every Wednesday to plant yourself under my desk. You have a decision to make, and you have about an hour before he drops you at the airport and leaves to go see the new victim."

Taylor walked away from me and my lungs began to burn. I hadn't realized I had been holding my breath until that moment. I gasped in the humid air and stared out at the water. I didn't know what to do.

I could give Mark his freedom by surrendering mine. I could give my dad back his life by giving myself to Taylor. I had been hard on my dad, too. For years, I thought he had killed someone for no reason only to find out he was merely saving Mark from a life of torment inside prison.

I wanted to call my dad at that moment and tell him I was sorry and beg his forgiveness. I wanted to tell him I loved him before it was too late. But I had turned in my phone so I couldn't be traced.

I grabbed the railing and held on tight as I climbed up and sat on the fence. I stared up at the sky and saw the flicker of one little star. It was sending Morse code down from Heaven, only I didn't understand it, so I was at a complete loss. All I knew was that my mom was with me at that moment.

"Brook." Mark called my name from behind me. "You're not going to jump, are you?" I could tell he was shaken from his phone call.

"And ruin my boots? No way." I smiled at him. He came up behind me and wrapped his arms around my waist. I wrapped my arms behind me to lay against his neck, and turned my head to kiss him. His coffee and whipped cream flavor flooded me, and I knew what I had to do.

"I am not going to go to the airport," I whispered.

"You're staying." Mark looked relieved.

"Taylor and I came to an understanding. You are going to be given immunity and my dad cleared. Plus, I am going to help the FBI catch the Cut-Me-Not killer."

Mark studied me intently. He knew there was more I wasn't saying. I could see his internal debate of asking whether or not he wanted to know.

"Brooklyn, men don't do things for free. What does Taylor get out of it?"

"Mark, do you really need to know? It's a way you and I can be together if you want me."

Mark's arms tightened around me and he breathed me in. I leaned my head back on his chest and stared at the star that flickered in the distance.

"Brooklyn, what do you have to give up for my freedom?" Mark asked in a rushed whisper.

"Myself."

"No. I won't let you. I am not worth that, Brooklyn." Mark let me go.

"Do you want to be with me?" I asked softly.

"More than my next breath. I want to marry you and have babies with you. I want to carry you on my arm everywhere we go so I can keep you safe and show you off. God, Brooklyn, I am nothing without you."

"Then to me, you are worth it." I jumped down off the rail, and wrapped my arms around him, telling him everything would be okay. I saw Taylor descending upon us quickly as I wrapped my arms around Mark's neck and pulled him down to me.

"Don't kill him. It's only sex in exchange for your freedom," I whispered into his ear.

"Are we headed to the airport?" Taylor asked, wanting to know if I had made a decision.

"No." Before Mark could interrupt, I covered his lips with my hand and started again. "I will stay, but we should go over the terms and conditions."

Taylor grinned and took his phone out. I heard him saying I was willing to work with the FBI before he stepped away and I couldn't hear him any longer.

"Brooklyn, don't do this for me. I can't ask you to do something like this," Mark said.

"You can give me something in exchange."

"What can I give you that would compare to what you are giving me?" Mark asked.

"Every night I come home to you after spending time with him. I want you to take me in the shower and scrub him off me. Then I want you to take me to bed and claim me as yours over and over again so his touch will become a distant memory and the only touch I will know will be yours."

Sorrow rushed through me for what he must be feeling. To have something you want but can't have unless what you want is sacrificed. It didn't seem fair when I thought of it that way

"Terms and conditions are as follows," Taylor started. "First, you answer to me and only me at the office. You earned your place there, so let me pick your cases. I will give you some tough ones, but I think you need to be challenged. Second, you will do whatever the FBI tells you to do. The director is flying back in two days to brief you over what they want you to do. You will be guarded as before, but it will be with fewer uniforms and more street clothes personnel."

Taylor stopped talking and looked at Mark. I nodded that he knew, inviting him to continue.

"I can have the paperwork signed and completed by morning for both Mark and your dad. After they have their walking papers, you belong to me. I may never call on you to do anything more than work longer hours, or I may call on you to be what I eat for lunch. I may call on you to paint the walls in my apartment. Whatever it is, you cannot say no, ever!"

It was my dream all over again. I was being fed to the devil when trying to stand up for someone else. I nodded my acknowledgment and pulled Mark back to the Escalade. We all gathered inside, and drove to the office so Taylor could get the paperwork done.

I sat on the top of my desk with Mark in between my legs. God, I loved this man. He brushed back my hair and kissed me lightly all over. It tickled and I began laughing as Taylor entered the room. It was nearing sun-up as I read over both sets of papers.

Mark signed his begrudgingly. Now it was time to call my dad.

I picked up the office phone and called, but I got his voicemail. Something caught my eye on the television in my office and I turned it up. We saw hundreds of people with black hair and blue eyes marching across the road, heading to the courthouse.

"Upon hearing the news of another two victims, the people have come together to show a united front against the killer."

They were chanting in the background. *"Stop Killing and Start the Healing."*

The newscaster even donned a black wig and continued the story, explaining that we would all look like those who are targeted so he wouldn't find another victim so easily.

CHAPTER
Thirteen

A WEEK HAD PASSED BY and I still had not heard from my dad. I left him voicemail after voicemail. We had gotten the signed papers back, so I knew he was all right, but something felt off.

Taylor had not asked for anything yet, but I never let my guard down. I was constantly in the courtroom or being briefed by the FBI. I accepted every piece of advice they threw my way except I was still going to wear my gun everywhere I went. Some days in the meetings, I envisioned putting a target on their backs and seeing how they liked being told they could not arm themselves.

The killer had taken out another two victims, but he had gotten people who were dressed like me. They weren't trying to be me like he had claimed. The crime scenes got messier, and the profiler said he was beginning to spiral out of control. He thought the killer would make a move against me soon.

I stacked papers on my desk when I heard a buzz from the intercom.

"Mr. Cross would like to see you in his office," my secretary said.

I pushed the button, accepting the message. I walked out the door and headed up a floor to the large conference room where Taylor had taken up residence as the case file became larger on this killer.

"Mr. Cross, you wanted to see me?" I asked quietly, never knowing what it was he wanted.

He took me by the elbow, leading me out of the conference room. We went down the hall, and inside the office next to his.

He immediately unbuttoned my shirt and pulled it off of me. He unzipped my skirt and let it fall. I was standing in the middle of the office wearing a white lace bra and white lace panties with black stiletto heels. I closed my eyes and imagined I was anywhere else.

I felt wind as he moved past me and heard the closet door open. I felt something scratch my skin as my hands were being tied together with braided rope in front of me. He must have done this before because the sailor's knot was nearly perfect.

Then he picked me up and carried me into the closet. I looked questioningly at him but said nothing.

"The closets are soundproof in case you scream or moan, since I know you are partial to both," he explained.

I took a deep breath. This is what I had agreed to. I took another deep breath, letting it out slowly.

"You nervous?" Taylor asked as I continued my deep breaths and stared at the rope that was marking my skin.

"A little," I admitted.

"Would you like your boyfriend to watch?" He turned on a monitor and the camera above it. "Do you want him to join?"

I shook my head. There was no way I could allow Mark to see what I was about to do. It would break his heart.

"What do I do now?" I asked. I had given myself to only a few men and understood what was expected, but when it was demanded it should come with instructions.

"You and Mark enjoy your day. You should start by expecting the worst and hoping for the best," Taylor explained in a rush. He opened the door, and Mark walked in. "You know, Ms. Montgomery, I would never force myself on anyone who didn't want me. You were willing and ready to go the distance to hold up your end of the bargain. I have to say it is noble, and one day I will be inside you again, but you will beg for it when it happens."

Surprising me, Taylor left the room. All of a sudden I was alone with Mark and a bunch of sex toys that said Taylor had a pervy side to him.

"I didn't want you to come for him. I didn't want you to ever have to do that for me." Mark pushed me against the wall. He wasted no time moving my underwear aside and pushing into me. His pants hadn't even hit the floor when I felt the burn of his entry.

The familiar stretch of him was comforting in the words he had just said. He was chaotic and everywhere at once. I pushed my face forward until his lips were locked with mine. He still covered every inch of me with his hands.

"Mark, I'm yours. Only yours. Now make me your bitch," I whispered with a grin, and bit his neck. I felt him smile as he pulled out and pushed back in. I moaned into the closet and winked up at the camera just for Taylor.

"Shouldn't you untie me so I can play, too?" I asked as he pulled me off the wall. He stopped and stared at me for a moment, realizing my hands were still bonded together by rope. He pulled out of me and set me on the ground. Unsteady on my legs, I dropped to my knees.

He pushed his cock near my face and I sucked it in as far as I could. I tried to reach up and wrap my hand around it, but it wasn't working.

"God, Brooklyn, that's good," Mark muttered as I worked twice as hard since I couldn't use my hands. I could taste me on him and it was a thrill to know he was mine and I was his. A new rush of moisture flooded my thighs. I needed him to come for me. I needed that renewed feeling of want. He tried to pull out as his cock swelled, but I sucked him and walked on my knees to follow.

"Brooklyn, I am going to come," Mark gritted through his teeth. I pulled back and smiled.

"So come, then." I sucked him back into my mouth and swallowed down on his cock. I watched as he fought on whether to grab my hair or the wall. He went for my hair and pushed me onto him as the first spurt flew. I swallowed it down in a rush and milked him for more. By the time I had licked him clean, he was out of breath and I was needy.

Mark pulled me over to a bench and bent me over it. I heard him grabbing for something and looked behind me to see he had a pink toy. I watched him turn it on and place it inside me. It was an egg that vibrated.

I sucked in air through my teeth as Mark climbed under the bench and watched my face. When I got close, he tugged the string and pulled it out. I whimpered and he placed it in me again. I quickly rode right back up the climax cliff for him to pull it out again. I thought I might die from a lack of orgasm.

My body tensed and my skin burned. I needed him. I needed this from him.

"Mark, please," I moaned.

"You beg so sweetly. Beg me. Tell me what you want."

"I want you inside me." I stuttered as he placed the egg back in me again. Then Mark put his finger in my mouth.

"Like this? You want me here? With my finger?" he asked, being a smart ass while I was a quivering ball of need.

"I need your cock inside me, please," I begged. Mark scooted out from under the bench and pulled the egg out once more. I was ready to scream in frustration.

I felt his tongue penetrate me and it began sliding in and out of me. I mewled with need. Then he placed the egg back inside me and turned the vibration to low.

I seethed the air in the room as he pulled me down to sit on his face. I was thanking God and seeing stars as I climbed back up the cliff. My stomach tightened and I clamped down on the egg. My toes curled and my heart raced. I screamed a guttural cry as I climaxed on his face.

Mark pulled the egg out and replaced it with his finger, hitting that rough patch and sending me higher. I needed to scratch or hit something, but my arms were bound together.

I tried to stand up and get away from his assaulting tongue, but he held me in place to take what he gave. He used his fingers to replace his tongue and pulled me down. I had asked him to claim me and that was exactly what he was doing. He pulled me down over the top of his cock and I lowered onto it slowly. My vaginal walls still tremored with the remnants of my orgasm.

"Take us home, baby," Mark whispered as he wiped the sweat off my brow. I placed my roped hands on his chest and pushed up off of him and lowered myself back down. I lifted a leg and spun on his cock to hear an intake of breath from Mark.

I leaned forward to get that one spot I knew and began riding him like a cowgirl. The new position had us both moaning. Mark grabbed my elbows and pulled me back a little to get more of him.

It wasn't long and my body was ready to go again. I clamped down on him and he released my elbows. He spanked my ass to cheer me along to get to the finish line. I tried to grab my breasts, but it wasn't working. I whimpered and Mark grabbed them for me. He pinched my nipples and kneaded them until I was crazy for release.

My vaginal walls began their tremors as Mark spun me back around. His hand went to the rope and held my hands as his fingers went to my clit. I screamed out in exhilaration as I crested over the cliff.

"Mark," I called out over and over. Tears shed from my eyes. I was wiped out by release. My body was numb other than the pulsating bundle of nerves at my apex. The orgasm rolled on and on through Mark's release and then some. Even when he stopped moving, I could still feel myself cresting again. If there was such a thing as death by orgasm I would have died then and there.

I dropped down on top of Mark, covered in sweat and ready for repair. Every strong orgasm Mark gave me seemed to chip away at the brick wall around my heart. Even though he was mine, I still guarded myself for fear he would change his mind.

Mark helped me up and helped me get dressed so we could go to dinner. As we headed out the door, I was suddenly feeling very off about my dad and wanted to see him. I had some kind of panic, thinking he might not be all right.

"Can I just meet you there?" I asked Mark.

"Why?" The detective in him appeared curious.

"I need to go to my dad's house."

"I will take you there. I have something I need to speak to him about, anyway."

Then entire drive, I sat staring at my hands. I wanted to chew my fingernails as the anxiety overwhelmed me. He had signed the papers, so he was fine. He just refused to return my phone calls.

As we pulled up to my dad's house, we rang the buzzer for the gate to open but no one opened it for us. I gave Mark the four digit code and the gates opened. The drive to the door was ominous, and I knew something was wrong.

We got out and rang the doorbell, but heard no movement. Mark pulled his gun and began walking around the porch, looking in the windows. I balled up my fist and beat on the door.

"Dad, open the door!" I screamed at the windows.

Mark was out of my sight for only a second when I heard a noise coming from the side. I pulled my gun and crept down by the pillar. I listened as the noise grew closer and closer. I nearly shot as our dog, Cricket, came around the corner. She whimpered as soon as she saw me and I pulled her to me. Her undercarriage was covered in blood and I saw a trail behind her.

I rubbed my hand down her chest to see she had a cut on her, but some of the blood was dry.

"Mark!" I screamed, and he came running up to me. He saw all the blood and picked up his phone and requested any available officers in the area and animal control. Mark crept around the side of the house following the blood trail while I stayed with Cricket on the porch. It was only minutes before police responded. Even the FBI pulled up front to help.

The FBI was always watching my dad, but apparently they were not watching close enough to see my dog get stabbed. Animal control rolled up and immediately took Cricket from me. I was covered in her blood as they carted her to the nearest vet.

I pulled my gun and picked up the extra key that was under a loose brick on the porch. I put the key in the hole and said a prayer that I would find him. I opened the door and saw a trail of blood inside. I walked just inside the door and to the left until I got past the stairs, then I walked slowly down the hallway. I turned the lock on the back door and edged my way out. When I came back to the front door, I looked down and saw my dad.

He was lying face down with his phone in hand behind the door. He had stab wounds that had been sewn shut and had begun to heal, as well as fresh ones still dripping with blood. I fell to my knees when I saw the little blue forget-me-not flowers all around his body.

I went to lunge for him when I was lifted off the floor. Taylor carried me outside and sat in the rocking chair on the porch with me in his lap as I cried my heart out. My dad had died and it had been my fault. I never told him I was sorry. I never told him I loved him.

Mark was out the door a few minutes later. He picked me up and placed me back inside his vehicle, then talked to Taylor for a few minutes. I watched, noticing they were both covered in blood and so was I. As officers roped off the pillars with yellow caution tape I saw the coroner's van and Doctor Garie pull up to the house.

I couldn't breathe. I felt like I was going to vomit. Mark and Taylor climbed into the vehicle and Taylor held me in the back seat. It felt like my life was ending in a daze.

We went to the police department where they collected our clothes as evidence. I was numb to the world. Everyone seemed to move in fast forward while I moved in slow motion. As they interviewed Mark and Taylor as to how they wound up at the house, I walked outside the precinct. I stared at the hustle and bustle of people moving on the street.

I was wearing an NYPD t-shirt and a pair of sweatpants with a pair of used running shoes they had found. My hair was still covered in blood and yet I didn't care. I started walking. I stared down at my shoes as I came to the crosswalk and nearly walked into an oncoming bus when someone grabbed my arm.

I slowly turned around to see light green eyes staring at me. I stood before him incapable of forming a conscious thought.

"Brooklyn?" He pulled me toward him. I went numbly to him and stood before him. Beaten down by emotions, I had nothing left.

"I take it you found your dad," the man stated, and I nodded, saying nothing.

"You brought this on yourself as you refused to play the *game*." He spoke as though I were a child. I stared right through him, and he let go. I started walking back toward the precinct. He didn't stop me. I guess I wasn't as much fun to play with anymore.

I was lost in my own head when he pulled my arm back, and I spun around. He planted his lips on mine and I stood before him numbly.

"What's your name?" I asked as he tried to kiss me.

"My name?" The killer's green eyes seemed to glow.

"I want to know the name of the person who is going to kill me," I whispered as the people flowed around us, not noticing our exchange.

"Call me R.J. But I told you, Brooklyn, I have no intentions to kill you unless you refuse to play along."

I stood before him like a zombie. I should have been angry. I should have been fighting for my life. But my grief ran too deep, and the guilt added to that kept all my other emotions at bay.

"Kill me," I whispered in his ear. "I don't want to live in a world where my friends and family are hunted down and murdered because you felt like I wasn't *playing* with you."

I pulled my arm away and turned my back on him. I thought he would end me then and there, but instead he disappeared into the crowd. As I stumbled back upon the police department, Mark ran for me, enveloping me in his arms.

"I'm so sorry," he exclaimed. "I'm so sorry. Tell me what you need."

That was the million dollar question. When my mom died, everyone asked what they could do. There is never anything a person can do. They are not God. They are not Jesus Christ. No one can bring my mom back, so why even ask. No one can bring my dad back, either.

Mark helped me into the Escalade and drove me to my apartment. I walked inside to find Kate waiting there. She had dyed her hair black and gotten blue contacts.

"Brook, I am so sorry," she muttered as she held me. She had tears streaming down her face, and I wondered why I couldn't do that.

"Kate, she is still in shock. And we just found her pacing outside the precinct," Mark explained.

They led me to the couch and I sat down as the doorbell rang. Taylor walked inside to get a briefing. I could hear them talking.

"The security footage shows Brooklyn with the suspect outside the precinct. He even saved her life. She went to step off the curb in front of a bus and he pulled her back," Taylor said.

"Did you bring the footage?" Mark asked.

I watched in slow motion as they headed into my bedroom. I stood up to follow, and Kate remained by my side. I watched behind them as they saw me walk out of the precinct. He had been waiting right beside the steps, and no one noticed him.

Then, when I uttered the words, "kill me," Mark turned his chair and looked at me.

"What did you say there, Brooklyn?" Mark asked.

"I can get a lip reader here in an hour if she isn't ready to talk about any of this," Taylor said.

"Brook, what did you say? I can read your lips, Brook, but I want you to tell me what you said," Mark demanded.

"I told him to kill me," I whispered. They fell silent for a long moment..

"Can you both give us the room for a minute?" Mark said to Taylor and Kate.

After he closed the door, I expected him to yell or be furious. Instead, he turned on my shower and carried me into the cold water. We were both still cold and I shrieked at the frigid temperature. I clawed at him to let me go.

"You finally ready to fight for your life, Brook?" Mark asked as the floodgates burst. I hung my head and cried into his chest. He reached behind us and warmed the shower.

Mark discarded my clothes and washed every inch of me. He even got the blood out of my hair. I held my stomach as I couldn't stop the tears. After I was clean, he turned off the water and carried me out. He wrapped a towel around me and discarded his clothes. He took my terrycloth robe and put it on, and then he dried me off.

He dressed me in fuzzy teal pajama pants and a teal tank top. He gathered up all the wet clothes and walked out of the bedroom to place them in the washer.

"Can we arrest him yet?" I asked Taylor in barely a whispered voice when I entered the living room.

"Brooklyn, I would love to say we have enough evidence. But it's all circumstantial, and with the new footage of him saving you, it makes him look like a hero, and not like the murdering bastard he is."

"Can everyone stay here with me tonight? You guys are the only family I have left and I want everyone together tonight."

Kate and Taylor both said yes. Mark wrapped his arms around me, and told me he and Taylor would go get some new clothes. They called in for a guard as I made sure my gun was loaded.

After they placed some young cop at my door, they left. Kate stayed with me as I tried to reel from the devastation I felt.

"How are you?" Kate asked.

"I never got to tell him I loved him," I replied with a sniffle.

"He knew, Brook. He always called Mark and I and made sure you were taken care of. He said you were too much like him. That you were too proud to express your feelings and too proud to ask for help."

That made me feel a little better about things, but it didn't change the fact that this psycho killed my dad.

"I should have gone there sooner, Kate. I could have done something."

"You mean like both of you dying together? Because that is the only thing that would've come of it."

Kate wrapped her arms around me and held me tight.

"You have to dye your hair back. I can't lose you, too," I murmured, and she nodded.

"This may be the wrong time, but I think a little change in subject is what we need right now. Do you want to tell me why your boss looks at you like you are his favorite little toy?"

"It's a long story."

"For something that is destined to be juicy, I have the time." Kate winked at me and gave me a crooked smile.

"Well…"

CHAPTER
Fourteen

T HREE DAYS HAD COME AND gone. Today was the day we would bury my dad. I expected it to be dark and gloomy, but the sun was shining as I woke up to a wonderful aroma in the apartment. Mark was sound asleep beside me, so I crept out of bed. I stepped into the kitchen to find Taylor cooking everyone breakfast.

"Need anything?" I asked, hoping I could do something to help.

"I'm good. How are you, darling?"

"I am as good as I am going to get, I think. Where's Kate?" I asked, looking around to see she hadn't come in last night.

"The ex-boyfriend called and wanted her to come over, so she went there and never came home," Taylor explained. "She will be at the funeral. She will probably be hung-over, but she will be there."

I climbed on the top of the island and Taylor came and stood between my legs. He glanced at me as if trying to see if I was okay.

"I have a sudden urge to kiss you," I whispered, and Taylor looked shocked.

"Not that I would stop you, but do you know why you feel this way?" he asked.

"I feel like my life is on a path to destruction and I need to alter my course. You might be the change I need."

Taylor went back and flipped the omelet he was making. I could see he was thinking about it.

"Look, Brooklyn, I would love to be balls deep inside you. I would love for you to kiss me, but you have a good man in there, and I think you should talk to him before you go altering your course."

I climbed off the island to find Mark standing behind the counter. He looked defeated. I walked up and took his hand and led him back to my bedroom.

"Is this the part where you tell me I am not enough? Mark asked.

I shook my head in response.

"Is this the part where you tell me you don't love me?" He crossed his arms and stared at me.

I shook my head again.

"Are you sleeping with him?" Mark asked, and from his stance I could tell he was preparing for the worst.

I shook my head yet again.

"Then what the hell was that about, Brooklyn?"

I lifted my head to look him in the eye. His beautiful cobalt eyes could drown me and steal my soul if I stared at them long enough.

"I was thinking this may be my last day on Earth," I replied. "The Marshals, the FBI, even the commissioner have said the same thing. They expect him to make a move on me at the funeral. I was thinking if I did something to change the future, to alter fate or destiny's course, then I would continue breathing tomorrow."

Mark stared intently at me before he began pacing.

"Let me get this straight. You want to have sex with Taylor as a change of pattern? Do you hear how it sounds? It sounds like the love of my life is going coo-coo for cocoa puffs." Mark spoke sarcastically.

"It was just a thought, Mark. If this were my last day on Earth, I would want my last moments to be with you. I just wondered what would happen if I changed something to change what we know is coming."

"Then you skip the funeral, you don't spread your legs for your boss!" Mark all but yelled.

I took a step back as the tears began to fall. He had been patient and understanding with me so far. I just needed him to see I didn't do anything wrong; it was merely a thought.

Mark opened the door and stormed out of our bedroom. Then I heard my front door slam. It was only a few minutes before I was being picked up off the floor by Taylor.

"I can't skip the funeral. It's my dad," I stuttered out through my cries.

Taylor merely held me there and rubbed his hand up and down my back. He kept whispering that I would be okay as I cried against him.

"I have an idea," Taylor said. "Kiss me, Brooklyn. You want to alter the events of today, and we still have an agreement. I own you. So kiss me."

I leaned up and looked at him in confusion. I applied my lips to his and kissed him. I didn't push it, and neither did he. It was a peck on the lips, nothing more. But it was at that moment that Mark walked back in.

All of a sudden he was pulling Taylor up and holding him by the throat.

"Mark, stop it!" I shrieked.

I watched as he slammed Taylor into the wall.

"Stop it!" I screamed again.

"Give me one reason I should let you live," Mark hissed at Taylor. I pulled my gun and slid back the slide. The noise rang out in my bedroom. I aimed it at Mark, and my heart shattered.

"Stop it!" I screamed and my knees hit the floor as the tears cascaded down my face. I gripped my chest as my heart broke.

Mark let go of Taylor and walked over to me. He took the gun from my hand. He emptied the clip and set the bullets and the gun on my desk.

"I'm sorry, Brooklyn. I can't do this with you anymore. I thought I could, but I can't. I can't share you, and you shouldn't want me to," Mark replied as he walked out the door.

Taylor lunged for me and enveloped me in his arms. The drywall in my apartment was broken, and so was my heart. I had loved him for twenty years, and now we were done. I was willing to trade my freedom for his, but when I needed a little compassion and understanding, he was ready to bail.

Taylor helped me up and brought me into the kitchen. He made me an omelet, but I wasn't hungry. I needed to get ready for the funeral. He locked the front door and gathered his suit and brought it into my bedroom. I heard the shower turn on and he came out for me.

"I swear, no hanky-panky, but we need to get ready and I don't want to leave you alone right now. Call me needy, but I want you to stay with me." Taylor gave me a half smile.

I got undressed slowly and climbed into the shower with him. He washed my hair as I washed my body. Once I was done, I climbed out. Then I watched as he washed and rinsed in under two minutes.

It amazed me how little time men spent getting ready. I began straightening my hair when Taylor walked out, a towel around his waist, his chiseled chest on display.

He took the brush and my straightener and straightened my hair for me without a word. Then he got dressed in his black suit and tie.

"Do you know what you're wearing?" Taylor asked.

I nodded, and pulled out a full-length black halter dress with a shawl. I had bought it just for my dad's funeral. I would probably burn it afterward, because I never wanted to wear it again.

"Taylor, if I die today, I want you to make sure they bury me in this." I pulled out a short sleeve lace dress. "It was my mom's wedding dress. I never had a husband or any children so it only seems appropriate that I get buried in it."

Taylor looked uncomfortable, but he nodded in agreement.

"How about we lay your dad to rest today, and get you out of there to fight another day."

Taylor was so sweet, but the evidence was there. The profilers and psych personnel all agreed this was going to be the killer's grand stand.

It always came back the same. He wanted to play a game with no rules, no instructions, no winners, and no losers. This wasn't a game to me. To him it was like chess, and any pawn who was on the board got wiped out.

Since I refused to play along, and had asked him to kill me on the street that day, I had taken myself off the board and that changed the game.

Now he was going to come for me so there would be a winner and a loser. The one who kept breathing would win. I swallowed hard as I thought about it. I had to give my father's eulogy and deal with being hunted by a psycho. On top of that, Mark had left me. Despite this, I still hadn't experienced a nervous breakdown.

I planted a kiss right on Taylor's lips. As soon as his mouth opened, I dove inside and tasted the caramel I had come to be familiar with. It wasn't coffee and whipped cream, but no one could replace Mark.

I wrapped my hands around the back of his neck and he pulled me close. I ran my fingers through his soft black hair, and dropped one hand down and placed it over his cock to rub through his clothes. Then he opened his emerald eyes and pushed my hands away.

"Brooklyn, you are upset right now. You are not thinking. In the morning, when Mark comes to apologize, you don't want to have done something you will feel guilty for. When you want me inside you, I will be there, but I want it to be because you want me, not because you are upset."

I felt mortified and suddenly very self-conscious. I put on my black strapless corset and clipped my thigh highs to my garter. Then I put on the bulletproof vest they had customized for another case. Once I put the dress on, it was impossible to tell I was wearing the vest. I put on my favorite strappy black heels.

I draped the shawl across my back, and grabbed my matching purse. I picked up my large black hat and placed it on my head. I looked like a million bucks and felt like scum.

I heard my doorbell as Taylor tied his shoes to get ready to go.

"Hi, Kate," I said as I opened the door. She came inside and saw Taylor in the bedroom and no Mark.

"You want to tell me what is written between the lines in the apartment right now?" Kate asked.

I told her what happened, and she scoffed at the situation.

"At least Taylor knew you were reacting as an emotional plane crash getting ready to happen. Mark yelled at you and left. You don't need this today. Wait until you look outside. It's amazing." Kate brought me to my window. "The news broke about your dad, and how you lost him to the killer you were trying to protect people from. They came forward."

I opened the window and looked down at all the people holding lit candles and singing Amazing Grace.

"Brooklyn, you stood up for your community and tried to do the right thing. You lost your dad from it. Now, the community wants to show they support you."

I stepped back and closed the window. I wasn't going to start crying and mess up my make-up. I fanned my face as we headed to the elevator.

Taylor stuck out his elbow and I took it. Kate stood right behind me in her black rockabilly dress. It was one my dad had bought her for her birthday a few years back, and it meant a lot to her. The elevator door opened, and we made our way out.

I was bombarded with hugs from strangers and people who said they were sorry. I never imagined anyone would care when my dad died because of who he was. Maybe they didn't care, but they felt my sorrow and that was refreshing. Sounds selfish, but I didn't want to be the only one in pain.

Taylor helped me push through the crowd and climb into the waiting limo. I leaned my head on Kate as I held Taylor's hand. I was grateful they were here, but they didn't offer up the same comfort Mark gave when I needed it. Upon arrival at the cemetery, there were officers and agents as far as the eye could see.

Kate climbed out first as the agents rushed the car. I didn't think my dad would be able to rest in peace while being swarmed by cops, but I wasn't ready to join him six feet under. I would leave them to their jobs and keep my lips zipped.

The officers swarmed me as I walked up the hill. My mom was buried under a cherry tree that overlooked part of the ocean. It was just outside the city in a quiet little suburb. I was having my dad laid to rest beside her. I saw the tent and chairs and went to take my seat. They had a bomb sniffing dog smell the chair prior to allowing me to sit.

Taylor's phone chimed an incoming text. I looked down and he cleared it quickly. I reached over and took his phone from him. I opened his text messages. This one was a blessing in disguise.

We have enough that I was able to ascertain a warrant this morning for R.J. Cummins. If you see him, they are to apprehend him and arrest him on eleven counts of murder and one charge attempted murder.

I handed Taylor his phone back. I scratched my head as the name sounded so familiar. I knew I didn't know him, but I had heard that name somewhere before.

"Eleven counts?" I asked, unaware of the added bodies.

"There were two that took place outside of the state. He will be charged and tried in—"

"Trenton," I finished for him. "In New Jersey."

Taylor stared at me as realization dawned on who he was.

"How did you know that?" he asked.

"Because I know where he lives."

"How the hell could you possibly know that?"

"His father killed Mark's mother. When my father was arrested, my mom used to take me out there to play with him while she helped his mom cook and clean. We were all friends until my mom got sick, and I stayed with Mark instead of going out there. The kid I used to play with...his name was Randy Junior Cummins."

Taylor started texting someone immediately, and the music began as the minister came forward. He preached about what an honorable man my dad was and then we bowed our heads to pray. After they finished the prayer, it was my turn to talk. I stood up in front of our family and friends and took a deep breath.

"My dad was a man who some were proud of, and a man some people feared."

I took a deep breath as I saw reporters writing every word I was saying.

"For those of you who were not invited...make sure you quote me correctly."

I picked up a red rose from the podium and smelled it as I prepared to say my final words about my dad.

"My dad was Nikolas Markovich, and what this city considered to be a Russian mobster. I won't lie and say I didn't question it when he went to prison, but he was always going to go to prison. The way the FBI stalked us, it was only a matter of time. I never saw the mobster in him. I saw a man who loved his family and chose to help those who couldn't help themselves. I loved my dad and respected him. I was his only daughter and it was an honor to have been the only daughter of Nikolas Markovich."

I walked forward and placed the rose on his casket. I looked up and saw Mark wearing his full dress policeman's uniform. I held my hand to the casket as if I couldn't walk away from him. I couldn't let them bury my dad just yet.

In a rushed reaction, I pushed the flowers off the casket. I went to open it when Mark scooped me up in his arms. I struggled with him as I needed to say I was sorry. But Mark started to carry me off when a voice shouted out above the crowd.

I looked up, and the green-eyed Cut-Me-Not killer, R.J., was standing at the foot of the casket.

"Let her say her peace with him." R.J.'s voice was firm. Mark set me down, but the radios went crazy and all the officers were called to another body. From the sounds on the radio, it was a lot more than just one body.

"I thought we needed some privacy for this," R.J. whispered, but I stood tall. I let him see defeat before, but not now.

"Why me?" I asked.

"Because you made the world love you. Then when someone loves you, you throw it away and disappear. You push us away the second you have our hearts. Then you ignore us and act as though we were never there."

Mark stood by my side. He was slowly moving to put himself between R.J. and me.

"I never wanted to hurt anyone, and I am sorry if I hurt you," I said. I saw Taylor texting someone, and Kate recording from the front row of chairs. My family was crying and unaware of who exactly RJ was.

"You do mean to hurt people. What did you do to Mark just this morning? You waited until he left, and put your lips on this guy over here." He waved his hand, and everyone looked at Taylor. "Then, as soon as Mark storms out, you do it again."

I felt Mark's heart break, but he stood stoic. He moved to cover part of me, but I merely stepped farther away. If I survived, at least I would get to see him behind bars.

"I know. I don't deserve him. I waited a very long time to be with him, and I wanted him to share me with Taylor *again!*" I replied.

R.J. looked like someone had punched him when I emphasized the word again. He pulled a gun from his jeans, and aimed it at me. Everyone murmured sounds of shock and fear. I put my hands up in a defensive manner and continued talking.

"I don't deserve Mark, but he will forgive me. That is what you do when you love someone. You forgive them for what they do. I could have slept with ten men this morning, and Mark would forgive me because we love each other enough to look past our mistakes."

Mark shot me a dirty look out of the corner of his eyes, and Taylor looked at me like I was speaking a foreign language. Kate understood. She nodded, knowing I was moving in the right direction.

"I think you loved me once, and I did something to hurt you. I also think you never forgave me for it. I think the reason you are killing all these women is because you are actually angry with me, and not the ones who look like me."

R.J.'s hands shook as he aimed the gun at me. He was having the internal conflict that I could see most men having when they had conversations with me.

"I can't forgive you. You left me alone with her while she drank herself to death and kept me locked away. The only time I existed was when we went to church and she threw water on me telling me my murdering father left the devil in me. When I needed you the most, you were in bed with Mark. We were seven years old, and you had already dismissed me for this guy." R.J. waved the gun at Mark.

"It's me you want to hurt, not him. If anyone has to die today, let it be me. Mark deserves better than me. He deserves a wife and babies. He deserves a happy life that ends in old age." I shouted above the gasping audience.

Sirens sounded in the background and the winds picked up as Mark began talking.

"I took her from you," Mark said. "I am the one you want. You already tried to kill me once, and had I not tripped, she would be yours again. If I were dead, what would stop her from going back to you?"

R.J. turned his head to Taylor and pointed the gun at him. Taylor stood with his hands up.

"It was a fantasy," he said. "That was all it was. She revealed a secret fantasy one night, and I stepped in so she didn't have to ask for it. It was one time. She has to choose who she wants to be with, and if she wants to be with Mark, she will. If she wants to be with me, she will. Have you asked her why she is not with you? Have you thought maybe the stack of dead bodies is part of the reason she wouldn't want to be with you? How could she ever trust you not to hurt her?"

I was standing behind the casket, which shielded my waist. R.J. pointed the gun at Mark, who was beside me. Then he pointed it at Taylor, who was moving in on the other side of me. Then the gun returned to me. The sirens grew louder and he was losing patience.

"Let me get you help, R.J.," I implored. "Let Mark take you in, and we can get you what you need." I spoke softly, but the words were all wrong.

"I'm not crazy!" he screamed, just before a shot rang out.

ABOUT THE
Author

AUTHOR ELIZABETH YORK HAS BEEN writing for about seven years. Located in the southeast, she spends her days drinking sweet tea on the porch with her laptop in hand. She has devoted her life to her family and her books. With the loss of her Father to cancer in 2010 she makes "Dear Daddy" dedication pages in each book and donates 10% royalties to cancer research.

Elizabeth was given a 2015 Author of the Year award sponsored by 31 blogs for her role in helping her fellow authors and her writing. She was also accepted into the Romance Writers of America organization in May of 2015.

For More Information:

www.facebook.com/authorlizyork
www.facebook.com/groups/LizYorkSreetTeam
www.facebook.com/groups/LizYorksFans
www.twitter.com/AuthorEYork
https://AuthorElizabethYork.com

CONTINUE
Reading The Series

Brooklyn's Survival—Book Two in the Brooklyn Series

Brooklyn Montgomery, was New York County's Assistant District Attorney. but sadly lost her life to join witness protection as a killer had targeted her. Brooklyn, can't handle the depressing life of witness protection and returns home.

Derrick Stevens, is a United States Marshal who has been charged with keeping Brooklyn hidden, but the killer sends her presents, until she can no longer deal with hiding. Upon her return home Derrick sticks around to watch as the life she thought she had unravels one person at a time.

Mark Stone, has always been the love of Brooklyn's life. From childhood friends to lovers these two have ran hot and cold as they try to determine their own boundaries,but upon

Brooklyn's return she meets Maya, Mark's girlfriend. With no warning he had moved on it sends her into the arms of Derrick Stevens, but something about him is off and she never lets her guard down.

Taylor Cross, is the District Attorney who betrayed Brooklyn and sent her into witness protection. Can she forgive him or will she use what he loves about her to manipulate him?

The adventure begins in an Applebee's in Texas where Brooklyn struggles to be Brooklyn and ends with ......

SURVIVED BY BROOKLYN—BOOK THREE IN THE BROOKLYN SERIES

Brooklyn Montgomery hasn't had the easiest life or done things the easy way. Her stubbornness sometimes outweighs her intelligence and forces bad choices. She deals with those choices head on, moving forward until she finds herself back at square one with no one she can trust when a new threat comes for her.

Mark Stone, once took a bullet for Brooklyn. He always forgave her, even overlooked her flaws. He was always there to catch her when she fell, but when he forgets who she is and has to start over will he find he has the same patience for her? Can he keep the killer away from her without knowing all the details?

What happens when both Brooklyn and Mark go missing? Will they be found, or will they be planted six feet under a field of forget-me-nots.